JUNIOR GREAT BOOKS

SERIES 5

SECOND SEMESTER

◆ ◆ ◆

AN INTERPRETIVE READING, WRITING,

AND DISCUSSION CURRICULUM

JUNIOR GREAT BOOKS

SERIES 5 SECOND SEMESTER

THE GREAT BOOKS FOUNDATION
A nonprofit educational corporation

ISBN 1-880323-07-9

9 8 7 6 5

Printed in the United States of America

Published and distributed by

THE GREAT BOOKS FOUNDATION
A nonprofit educational corporation

35 East Wacker Drive, Suite 2300

Chicago, IL 60601-2298

Contents

PREFACE

SHARED INQUIRY: A REVIEW

This is the beginning of your second semester of Junior Great Books. You and the others in your class will again be reading stories, writing questions about them, and discussing them. As you know, Junior Great Books offers you an opportunity to think for yourself about the meanings a story can have and to build upon your ideas through *shared inquiry.* To take an active part in shared inquiry you will be reading the stories twice, making notes and thinking of questions as you read. When your class discusses the story, you will need to listen closely so that you can respond to the questions that your teacher or leader asks and to the questions and ideas of your classmates.

In shared inquiry, thoughtful readers come together to interpret the meaning of a story. Leaders do not know the answers to the interpretive questions they ask. They are not waiting to hear one particular answer; they hope to discover several good answers. A good answer is a logical one that can be backed up with evidence from the story; any answer you give is a good one if it helps to make sense of the story. As you participate in shared inquiry, you will develop your own interpretation of what you read. You will be working to discover what the author wants to tell you or make you feel through his or her words.

Shared Inquiry Discussion is guided by these four rules:

1. **Only people who have read the story may take part in Shared Inquiry Discussion.**

2. **Discuss only the story everyone has read.**

3. **Do not use other people's opinions about the story unless you can back them up with evidence of your own.**

4. **Leaders may only ask questions; they may not answer them.**

INTERPRETIVE QUESTIONS

Some stories are simple and easy for us to understand. Others are more perplexing. In this second kind of story the author is trying to share with us ideas and feelings that are not obvious or easy to describe. You can fully understand such stories only if you actively seek their meaning out by asking questions.

As you read the stories in Junior Great Books, many questions will probably occur to you. Some of these questions will be factual, and in many cases a first reading of the story will answer them for you.

But other questions that occur to you will not be answered by the first reading. You may continue to wonder about these questions, and you may not find an answer that really satisfies you. You will need to look actively for the answers when you read the story again.

Questions that you cannot answer after the first reading are probably good interpretive questions. The second reading will help you bring these questions into focus and begin to look for possible answers to them.

In shared inquiry, you will need to read with a pencil in hand and to make notes as you read. While you are reading, mark the words and passages in the story that strike you as really important, interesting, or surprising. Mark places that make you think of a question. Mark parts that give you ideas about what the story means. Your teacher or leader may also ask you to watch for particular things during your reading and to give them special attention. Your notes will remind you of your thoughts while reading and help you to find evidence to back up what you say.

Remember that in shared inquiry there are three kinds of questions:

Questions of fact ask you to recall particular details or events from a story. They have only one correct answer.

Questions of interpretation ask you to think carefully about what happens in a story and to consider what the story means. Interpretive questions have more than one good answer that can be supported with what is said in the story.

Questions of evaluation ask how the story fits with your own experience and, after you have interpreted it, whether or not you agree with what the story is saying.

Writing interpretive questions is one of the best ways to think on your own about the meaning of a story. Reading is not just a search for answers; it is also a search for new questions that you might want to raise. These are very often interpretive questions, some of which you may decide would be good to discuss. Here are some good sources of interpretive questions:

Words or passages that you think are important and that you wonder about

Parts of the story that you feel strongly about

Your curiosity about the characters

Your ideas about the story's meaning

ACTIVE LISTENING

When you think of discussing the stories in Junior Great Books, you probably think first of speaking—of answering the questions the leader asks. But most of the time you will be listening, not speaking.

Good listening is essential to good discussion. In shared inquiry, members of the group learn from one another by sharing questions, comparing notes, and exchanging ideas in response to questions. A response you hear from one of your classmates may prompt a new idea in you. By sharing this idea, you can prompt yet another idea in someone who is listening to you. As you listen to one another and explain your ideas to one another, the members of your group will discover new meanings in the story you have read. Discussion in Junior Great Books becomes like a conversation between friends who, because they listen closely to each other, can think thoughts together that they could not have thought alone.

Like good reading, good listening is active and responsive. When you exchange opinions with other members of your class you may feel surprise or excitement. You may strongly agree or disagree. And sometimes you will need to wait for a while to decide what you think. The first thing you notice as you listen may be whether the other person is agreeing with something you have said. But you will also want to understand *why* that person agrees or disagrees.

In shared inquiry, you have the opportunity to listen to the ideas of others and to respond. Like the leader, you may ask the others questions about what they have said. If you are not sure of what you think about a new idea that someone has put forward, asking questions is a good way to make things clearer. If you are sure, you can tell the person why you agree or disagree, backing up what you say with evidence from the text. Your questions and comments will help the group understand this participant better and lead everyone more deeply into the story.

Remember to look at your classmates when you are talking. This will help them pay close attention to what you say.

Good listening is a skill that takes time to learn. It isn't easy to follow everything that is said. It takes patience to listen to others and not to break in when they are trying to put their thoughts into words. When you are a good listener, you will not only be eager to discuss your own ideas. You will also be ready to respond thoughtfully to the ideas of others.

A Game of Catch

Richard Wilbur

Monk and Glennie were playing catch on the side lawn of the firehouse when Scho caught sight of them. They were good at it, for seventh-graders, as anyone could see right away. Monk, wearing a catcher's mitt, would lean easily sidewise and back, with one leg lifted and his throwing hand almost down to the grass, and then lob the white ball straight up into the sunlight. Glennie would shield his eyes with his left hand and, just as the ball fell past him, snag it with a little dart of his glove. Then he would burn the ball straight toward Monk, and it would spank into the round mitt and sit, like a still-life apple on a plate, until Monk flipped it over into his right hand and, with a negligent flick of his hanging arm, gave Glennie a fast grounder.

They were going on and on like that, in a kind of slow, mannered, luxurious dance in the sun, their faces perfectly blank and entranced, when Glennie noticed Scho dawdling along the other side of the street and called hello to him. Scho crossed over and stood at the front edge of the lawn, near an apple tree, watching.

"Got your glove?" asked Glennie after a time. Scho obviously hadn't.

"You could give me some easy grounders," said Scho. "But don't burn 'em."

"All right," Glennie said. He moved off a little, so the three of them formed a triangle, and they passed the ball around for about five minutes, Monk tossing easy grounders to Scho, Scho throwing to Glennie, and Glennie burning them in to Monk. After a while, Monk began to throw them back to Glennie once or twice before he let Scho have his grounder, and finally Monk gave Scho a fast, bumpy grounder that hopped over his shoulder and went into the brake on the other side of the street.

"Not so hard," called Scho as he ran across to get it.

"You should've had it," Monk shouted.

It took Scho a little while to find the ball among the ferns and dead leaves, and when he saw it, he grabbed it up and threw it toward Glennie. It struck the trunk of the apple tree, bounced back at an angle, and rolled steadily and stupidly onto the cement apron in front of the firehouse, where one of the trucks was parked. Scho ran hard and stopped it just before it rolled under the truck, and this time he carried it back to his former position on the lawn and threw it carefully to Glennie.

"I got an idea," said Glennie. "Why don't Monk and I catch for five minutes more, and then you can borrow one of our gloves?"

"That's all right with me," said Monk. He socked his fist into his mitt, and Glennie burned one in.

"All right," Scho said, and went over and sat under the tree. There in the shade he watched them resume their skillful play. They threw lazily fast or lazily slow—high, low, or wide—and always handsomely, their expressions serene, changeless, and forgetful. When Monk missed a low backhand catch, he walked indolently after the ball and, hardly even looking, flung it sidearm for an imaginary put-out. After a good while of this, Scho said, "Isn't it five minutes yet?"

"One minute to go," said Monk, with a fraction of a grin.

Scho stood up and watched the ball slap back and forth for several minutes more, and then he turned and pulled himself up into the crotch of the tree.

"Where are you going?" Monk asked.

"Just up the tree," Scho said.

"I guess he doesn't want to catch," said Monk.

Scho went up and up through the fat light-gray branches until they grew slender and bright and gave under him. He found a place where several supple branches were knit to make a dangerous chair, and sat there with his head coming out of the leaves into the sunlight. He could see the two other boys down below, the ball going back and forth between them as if they were bowling on the grass, and Glennie's crew-cut head looking like a sea urchin.

"I found a wonderful seat up here," Scho said loudly. "If I don't fall out." Monk and Glennie didn't look up or comment and so he began jouncing gently in his chair of branches and singing "Yo-ho, heave ho" in an exaggerated way.

"Do you know what, Monk?" he announced in a few moments. "I can make you two guys do anything I want. Catch that ball, Monk! Now you catch it, Glennie!"

"I was going to catch it anyway," Monk suddenly said. "You're not making anybody do anything when they're already going to do it anyway."

"I made you say what you just said," Scho replied joyfully.

"No, you didn't," said Monk, still throwing and catching but now less serenely absorbed in the game.

"That's what I wanted you to say," Scho said.

The ball bounded off the rim of Monk's mitt and plowed into a gladiolus bed beside the firehouse, and Monk ran to get it while Scho jounced in his treetop and sang, "I wanted you to miss that. Anything you do is what I wanted you to do."

"Let's quit for a minute," Glennie suggested.

"We might as well, until the peanut gallery shuts up," Monk said.

They went over and sat crosslegged in the shade of the tree. Scho looked down between his legs and saw them on the dim, spotty ground, saying nothing to one another. Glennie soon began abstractedly spinning his glove between his palms; Monk pulled his nose and stared out across the lawn.

"I want you to mess around with your nose, Monk," said Scho, giggling. Monk withdrew his hand from his face.

"Do that with your glove, Glennie," Scho persisted. "Monk, I want you to pull up hunks of grass and chew on it."

Glennie looked up and saw a self-delighted, intense face staring down at him through the leaves. "Stop being a dope and come down and we'll catch for a few minutes," he said.

Scho hesitated, and then said, in a tentatively mocking voice, "That's what I wanted you to say."

"All right, then, nuts to you," said Glennie.

"Why don't you keep quiet and stop bothering people?" Monk asked.

"I made you say that," Scho replied, softly.

"Shut up," Monk said.

"I made you say that, and I want you to be standing there looking sore. And I want you to climb up the tree. I'm making you do it!"

Monk was scrambling up through the branches, awkward in his haste, and getting snagged on twigs. His face was furious and foolish, and he kept telling Scho to shut up, shut up, shut up, while the other's exuberant and panicky voice poured down upon his head.

"Now you shut up or you'll be sorry," Monk said, breathing hard as he reached up and threatened to shake the cradle of slight branches in which Scho was sitting.

"I *want*—" Scho screamed as he fell. Two lower branches broke his rustling, crackling fall, but he landed on his back with a deep thud and lay still, with a strangled look on his face and his eyes clenched. Glennie knelt down and asked breathlessly, "Are you OK, Scho? Are you OK?" while Monk swung down through the leaves crying that honestly he hadn't even touched him, the crazy guy just let go. Scho doubled up and turned over on his right side, and now both the other boys knelt beside him, pawing at his shoulder and begging to know how he was.

Then Scho rolled away from them and sat partly up, still struggling to get his wind but forcing a species of smile onto his face.

"I'm sorry, Scho," Monk said. "I didn't mean to make you fall."

Scho's voice came out weak and gravelly, in gasps. "I meant—you to do it. You—had to. You can't do—anything—unless I want—you to."

Glennie and Monk looked helplessly at him as he sat there, breathing a bit more easily and smiling fixedly, with tears in his eyes. Then they picked up their gloves and the ball, walked over to the street, and went slowly away down the sidewalk, Monk punching his fist into the mitt, Glennie juggling the ball between glove and hand.

From under the apple tree, Scho, still bent over a little for lack of breath, croaked after them in triumph and misery, "I want you to do whatever you're going to do for the whole rest of your life!"

THE TALE OF THE THREE STORYTELLERS

James Krüss

In olden times there lived three storytellers in the town of Usküb, who made a living, more or less, from their talents. Every day they went to the Bazaar to gather some listeners and maybe make a few piasters. But since at that time trade had become more and more difficult (bands of robbers lay in ambush for the merchants), all wares had become expensive, and money had become scarce. The three storytellers could hardly make enough to feed their families.

Finally they decided that only one of them should tell stories and the other two should try to make a living by becoming bath attendants or water boys. All three agreed, and shook hands on it, that the one who was able to gather the most listeners for a story during the next three days would continue as the storyteller. They further agreed to tell only stories about thieves.

The following day the first storyteller, named Achmed-with-the-Long-Chin, went to the Bazaar to try his luck. He looked tired and cross, because he had spent the whole night wondering how to start his story in order to get as many listeners as possible right at the beginning. And only in the early morning, as the roosters were crowing, did he think of a beginning that he felt would be effective.

The other two storytellers, Ibraim-the-Pumpkinhead and Jussuf-of-Bagdad, were already at the Bazaar when Achmed-with-the-Long-Chin arrived to tell his story.

"People," shouted Achmed as loud as he could. "Look at me. I am the master thief of Usküb! Last night I stole the hair off a man's head without his knowing it, and I will tell you how I did it!"

The people at the Bazaar came closer and laughed, because the theft of a man's hair promised to make a funny story.

But, as fate would have it, just at that time a hair-sickness had spread in Usküb, and more than one man had lost his hair overnight. Each of these bald-headed people—and by now there were at least twenty or thirty at the Bazaar—seriously believed that Achmed-with-the-Long-Chin had stolen his hair. A murderous shout arose. The baldheads took their turbans and fezzes off and screamed, "Look what he did to us, the miserable thief, the disgraceful pirate! And he dares to brag about his scandalous doings! Get him, get him and beat him up! He shall suffer for this!"

Twenty or thirty baldheads stormed on Achmed, and a lot of people followed them, partly in anger and partly because they liked a good fight.

When Achmed-with-the-Long-Chin saw that they were really serious, he shouted, "Stop! Stop! I was only telling a story! I am only pretending to be a thief!"

"By Allah, now he starts to lie!" shouted the baldheads. "But by the beard of the prophet, that shall not avail him!"

They grabbed the storyteller, who was scared to death, and beat him up. It was something to see. Ibraim-the-Pumpkinhead and Jussuf-of-Bagdad, the other two storytellers, tried to come to the aid of their friend and clear up the mistake. But there was no holding the mob. Achmed-with-the-Long-Chin was first beaten to a pulp and then dragged to a barber who shaved all the hair off his head. He looked so strange that laughter began that sounded as if it would never end. After awhile, when it became known that poor Achmed was really not a thief but had only wanted to attract listeners, the laughter grew even louder than it had been. Ever since that time there has been a saying in Usküb: "If you have stolen someone's hair, watch out for baldheads."

Achmed-with-the-Long-Chin looked like a plucked owl after his adventure at the Bazaar. And his story was never told.

The next morning Ibraim-the-Pumpkinhead tried his luck. In the meantime the news had spread around town that Usküb's three storytellers were having a contest among themselves, and this time a lot of curious and fun-loving people were gathered at the Bazaar.

Ibraim-the-Pumpkinhead had decided to start by addressing his audience very politely before he began with the real story; he had learned from the experience of Achmed-with-the-Long-Chin that it is very important to keep the audience on your side. So he began as follows:

"Allah be with you, my friends! I am Ibraim, called the Pumpkinhead because right after I was born an oil lamp fell on my little head."

"Hear, hear!" shouted the listeners. "He is going to tell us the story of the Pumpkinhead. That could be funny!"

Ibraim continued, "Allah is great! He did give me a pumpkinhead, but above my left eye, where the imagination is located, he blew into me the beautiful talent of storytelling so that I might amuse my friends at the Bazaar."

"What kind of story is he telling us?" the listeners asked one another. "You can't tell what he is trying to say!"

Ibraim continued, "I never really learned the art of storytelling, my friends. It was bestowed upon me from Heaven."

"Maybe it came down with the oil lamp," shouted one of the listeners, and there was a first ripple of laughter. This confused Ibraim-the-Pumpkinhead greatly. He decided to start his story immediately so as not to be ridiculed a second time. He went on quickly, "Allah is great, and Mohammed is his prophet! The story that I am going to tell you today concerns a very special thief!"

"Tell us the story of the thief who stole hair at night!" they shouted at him laughingly.

"Allah be with me," said Ibraim-the-Pumpkinhead. "I would like to get home in one piece!"

Now he had the jokers on his side, but his audience had meanwhile grown restless, because they still did not know what kind of special thief he was going to talk about. Some started to leave, others talked loudly to each other about the high prices charged by the insolent merchants, and still others amused themselves poking fun at Ibraim.

One of them shouted, "Tell us the story of the thief who stole with his feet!"

Another one wanted to hear the story of the louse-thief. Ibraim-the-Pumpkinhead grew restless. He shouted, "I don't know that story! But I promise you a story that is just as entertaining! Even though it is a long story, it is a very beautiful story. It begins at the Bazaar in Bagdad where I was myself, more than ten years ago, and it ends right here in Usküb."

This announcement of Ibraim's made the people very cross, because the road from Bagdad to Usküb is long and nobody wants to stand around and hear a story of such length.

So most of the listeners went away to enjoy Turkish coffee and a good game of dominoes. At least you could sit down doing that. Only a few listeners remained to have their fun with Ibraim.

They shouted, "What did you do in Bagdad? Did you buy oil for your little lamp?"

Again there was laughter, but now Ibraim had had enough.

"Foolish people!" he screamed. "Can't you wait quietly until I start my story? Didn't your whipping masters bring you up properly? Be quiet and listen!"

With this, the trouble really started.

"Look at him, that Pumpkinhead!" they shouted. "First he does not begin his story, and then he blames us because he did not start! What kind of sense is that?"

The people were really angry at Ibraim now, and all of a sudden, from nowhere, a melon flew at him. As fate would have it, Ibraim was standing right below a coppersmith's display shelf, and the melon knocked down three oil lamps. These oil lamps fell on his head, one after another, so that first he saw stars, then the moon, and finally thirty-seven suns dancing in front of his eyes; and he began to turn around and around, bawling.

The people shouted, "The Pumpkinhead is dancing!" And they clapped their heads and doubled up in laughter. Still laughing, and wanting more amusement because the story had been such a disappointment, the crowd turned for more melons. Another and another and another reached the unfortunate Ibraim.

Jussuf-of-Bagdad, the third storyteller, was the only one who did not laugh. He grabbed the hopping, twirling Ibraim by his caftan, which is a Turkish robe, and dragged him past the jeering crowd, through the whole Bazaar to his home.

Ever since that time, people in Usküb have said of anybody who has difficulty expressing himself: "Three oil lamps must have hit him on the head."

Poor Ibraim now ran around with three big lumps on his head; he looked like a pumpkin with three horns.

The morning after Ibraim's adventure, Jussuf-of-Bagdad went to the Bazaar to entertain the people with his story about thieves. He had not prepared any special beginning nor pleasant introduction. He planned to draw the people just with his story. And since he knew exactly how the story was going to end, he had no trouble finding a beginning.

This time the crowd of curiosity seekers was, if possible, even greater than it had been the day before, and hidden way back in a corner squatted the shorn Achmed-with-the-Long-Chin and Ibraim-with-the-Swollen-Pumpkinhead.

At first Jussuf-of-Bagdad did not say a word. He sat in a carpet dealer's stall, his arms crossed, and looked at his listeners silently until the whole Bazaar was as quiet as a mouse and everyone stared at him in suspense. Then he calmly began to tell his story:

THE CALIPH AND THE BARBER

One night as Harun al Raschid, the great Caliph, sauntered through the darkening city of Bagdad in disguise, a yearning for roasted chestnuts came over him.

Approaching a chestnut vendor, he realized he had forgotten to bring any money along. But a Caliph is not used to forgoing his desires, so Harun al Raschid got his chestnuts even without any money. He picked up a stone from the street and threw it quickly against an iron door as he was passing the chestnut stand. A mighty bang sounded through the dark street, and the chestnut vendor turned around in fright. The Caliph used this moment to steal a handful of chestnuts. He hid them under his caftan and calmly continued his walk, not betraying himself by hurrying.

When he began to eat the chestnuts, he noticed that he had lost a precious ring while stealing. "Expensive chestnuts!" he murmured.

Soon thereafter, the Caliph felt a yearning for Turkish honey. And at the same moment he saw a honey seller standing at a street corner next to a little fire.

A Caliph is not used to forgoing his desires, so Harun al Raschid got his honey even without any money. As he was passing the honey seller, he quickly threw the shells of his chestnuts into the fire; that made the fire crackle and hiss so that the honey seller quickly jumped aside and stared fearfully into the excited flames.

The Caliph used this moment to quickly break off a piece of Turkish honey. He hid it under his caftan and strode on in dignity, as if nothing had happened.

A little further down the road when he pulled the honey out from under his caftan, he noticed that he had lost his precious dagger while stealing. "Expensive honey!" he murmured.

Again, a little while later, he yearned for cherries. A Caliph is not used to forgoing his desires, so Harun al Raschid got his cherries even without any money. He slowly sauntered into a dark alley, brushed as if by chance against a garden fence, and stole, in passing, a handful of cherries from a tree. He hid them under his caftan.

But when he began to eat the cherries, a little later, he noticed that he had lost a precious earring while stealing. "Expensive cherries!" he murmured.

The next day, as the Caliph was sitting in full regalia in his palace, he had a herald announce that he had lost a ring, a dagger, and an earring, promising a high reward to the finder. He was hoping that the chestnut vendor, the honey seller, and the owner of the garden would come to him so that he could pay them for the stolen goods.

But not one of the three came. Instead, the valuables were found several weeks later at the home of a young barber, who was immediately put in irons and led before the Caliph.

"How did you get my jewelry?" demanded the Caliph of the barber.

"Forgive me, O Ruler of all Faithful," answered the young man with downcast eyes. "I took them from you in concern for your well-being!"

This answer surprised the court, but even more the Caliph himself.

"Explain that in a little more detail, young fellow!" he said.

"Now then, O great Caliph, know ye that I took the ring from you at the chestnut vendor for fear it might get caught and thus give you away!"

Again the court was astounded at this answer. The only one who was not astounded was the Caliph. He is even supposed to have smiled.

The barber went on: "The dagger, O Ruler of all Faithful, I took from you at the Turkish honey seller. How easily it might have hit the iron table and given you away!"

"And how about the earring, my good man?"

The court was amazed to hear the Caliph address a simple barber as "my good man." But the young man only said, "The earring, O great Caliph, I had to take from you at the cherry tree, for it might have caught on a branch and torn your ear lobe."

At these words the whole court shook its head in amazement. But Harun al Raschid rose, took the irons off the barber with his own hands, and said, "Since you did all this in concern for my well-being, you shall be free, master barber. But do tell me this: How was it possible that I did not see you?"

"I walked in your shadow, my lord. That is what I was taught. For our trade too has to be learned, and it takes long practice before one becomes a master!"

"Since I neither heard you nor saw you that night, you really must be a master-er barber!" said the Caliph with a sidelong glance at his court. "So do go home and take my precious jewelry along as a gift. But watch your tongue and make your living from now on by being just a barber. Should your talent be of use to me, though, I shall remember you! Allah be with you!"

"May Allah bless Harun al Raschid, the Ruler of all Faithful!" answered the young barber, bowing deeply. Then he left the palace unhindered, taking the Caliph's dagger, ring, and earring with him.

Amazed, the courtiers asked, "Why, O great Caliph, did you bestow such honor on a thieving barber?"

"Because a thief cannot sit in judgment on a thief," said the Caliph. "And because he shows talents that astound me!"

Not once had the listeners at the Bazaar of Usküb interrupted the storyteller, Jussuf-of-Bagdad, as he told his story. They had been as quiet as robbers in a bush when a merchant passes by. And now they applauded long and loudly, shook Jussuf's hand, and said, "That was really an excellent thief story. You entertained us grandly!"

They were about to leave, giving him but a single piaster.

But Jussuf-of-Bagdad called out to them: "Dear friends, if you do not pay a storyteller, he might have to change his trade and become a thief. That would be bad for the storyteller and bad for your precious snuff boxes. Think about it—would you rather have me as a storyteller or as a thief?"

Suddenly many people noticed that their richly ornamented snuff boxes had been stolen from the pockets of their caftans. They looked at each other suspiciously, realized all at once who the thief was, and began to laugh so heartily that it could be heard all the way up to gypsy-town.

"By Allah, what a man!" they shouted. "He tells us an exciting thief story, and when we come close out of curiosity and excitement, he calmly steals our snuff boxes. And nobody notices anything! What a man!"

A heavyset emir with a grass-green turban shouted, "Give us back our snuff boxes, Jussuf! You shall have your money!"

At that Jussuf-of-Bagdad pulled twenty-four snuff boxes from under his crossed legs and gave them back to their owners. Piasters began to rain on the carpet on which he was sitting.

Ever since that time there has been a saying in Usküb: "Where poets get paid, thieves become honest!"

The two other storytellers, Achmed-with-the-Long-Chin and Ibraim-the-Pumpkinhead, gaped open-mouthed at the artfulness of their friend, and gave him, without grudge, the position of storyteller at the Bazaar. Achmed became a water boy and Ibraim earned his living as a bath attendant.

Allah gave them all a long and happy life. Sela.

SPIT NOLAN

Bill Naughton

Spit Nolan was a pal of mine. He was a thin lad with a bony face that was always pale, except for two rosy spots on his cheekbones. He had quick brown eyes, short, wiry hair, rather stooped shoulders, and we all knew that he had only one lung. He had had a disease which in those days couldn't be cured, unless you went away to Switzerland, which Spit certainly couldn't afford. He wasn't sorry for himself in any way, and in fact we envied him, because he never had to go to school.

Spit was the champion trolley-rider of Cotton Pocket; that was the district in which we lived. He had a very good balance, and sharp wits, and he was very brave, so that these qualities, when added to his skill as a rider, meant that no other boy could ever beat Spit on a trolley—and every lad had one.

Our trolleys were simple vehicles for getting a good ride downhill at a fast speed. To make one you had to get a stout piece of wood about five feet in length and eighteen inches wide. Then you needed four wheels, preferably two pairs, large ones for the back and smaller ones for the front. However, since we bought our wheels from the scrapyard, most trolleys had four odd wheels. Now you had to get a poker and put it in the fire until it was red hot, and then burn a hole through the wood at the front. Usually it would take three or four attempts to get the hole bored through. Through this hole you fitted the giant nut-and-bolt, which acted as a swivel for the steering. Fastened to the nut was a strip of wood, on to which the front axle was secured by bent nails. A piece of rope tied to each end of the axle served for steering. Then a knob of margarine had to be slanced out of the kitchen to grease the wheels and bearings. Next you had to paint a name on it: *Invincible* or *Dreadnought,* though it might be a motto: *Death before Dishonour,* or *Labour and Wait.* That done, you then stuck your chest out, opened the back gate, and wheeled your trolley out to face the critical eyes of the world.

Spit spent most mornings trying out new speed gadgets on his trolley, or searching Enty's scrapyard for good wheels. Afterwards he would go off and have a spin down Cemetery Brew. This was a very steep road that led to the cemetery, and it was very popular with trolley-drivers as it was the only macadamized hill for miles around, all the others being cobblestones for horse traffic. Spit used to lie in wait for a coal-cart or other horse-drawn vehicle, then he would hitch *Egdam* to the back to take it up the brew. *Egdam* was a name in memory of a girl called Madge, whom he had once met at Southport Sanatorium, where he had spent three happy weeks. Only I knew the meaning of it, for he had reversed the letters of her name to keep his love a secret.

It was the custom for lads to gather at the street corner on summer evenings and, trolleys parked at hand, discuss trolleying, road surfaces, and also show off any new gadgets. Then, when Spit gave the sign, we used to set off for Cemetery Brew. There was scarcely any evening traffic on the roads in those days, so that we could have a good practice before our evening race. Spit, the unbeaten champion, would inspect every trolley and rider, and allow a start which was reckoned on the size of the wheels and the weight of the rider. He was always the last in the line of starters, though no matter how long a start he gave it seemed impossible to beat him. He knew that road like the palm of his hand, every tiny lump or pothole, and he never came a cropper.

Among us he took things easy, but when occasion asked for it he would go all out. Once he had to meet a challenge from Ducker Smith, the champion of the Engine Row gang. On that occasion Spit borrowed a wheel from the baby's pram, removing one nearest the wall, so it wouldn't be missed, and confident he could replace it before his mother took baby out. And after fixing it to his trolley he made that ride on what was called the "belly-down" style—that is, he lay full stretch on his stomach, so as to avoid wind resistance. Although Ducker got away with a flying start he had not that sensitive touch of Spit, and his frequent bumps and swerves lost him valuable inches, so that he lost the race with a good three lengths. Spit arrived home just in time to catch his mother as she was wheeling young Georgie off the doorstep, and if he had not made a dash for it the child would have fallen out as the pram overturned.

It happened that we were gathered at the street corner with our trolleys one evening when Ernie Haddock let out a hiccup of wonder: "Hey, chaps, wot's Leslie got?"

We all turned our eyes on Leslie Duckett, the plump son of the local publican. He approached us on a brand-new trolley, propelled by flicks of his foot on the pavement. From a distance the thing had looked impressive, but now, when it came up among us, we were too dumbfounded to speak. Such a magnificent trolley had never been seen! The riding board was of solid oak, almost two inches thick; four new wheels with pneumatic tyres; a brake, a bell, a lamp, and a spotless steering-cord. In front was a plate on which was the name in bold lettering: *The British Queen.*

"It's called after the pub," remarked Leslie. He tried to edge it away from Spit's trolley, for it made *Egdam* appear horribly insignificant. Voices had been stilled for a minute, but now they broke out:

"Where'd it come from?"

"How much was it?"

"Who made it?"

Leslie tried to look modest. "My dad had it specially made to measure," he said, "by the gaffer of the Holt Engineering Works."

He was a nice lad, and now he wasn't sure whether to feel proud or ashamed. The fact was, nobody had ever had a trolley made by somebody else. Trolleys were swopped and so on, but no lad had ever owned one that had been made by other hands. We went quiet now, for Spit had calmly turned his attention to it and was examining *The British Queen* with his expert eye. First he tilted it, so that one of the rear wheels was off the ground, and after giving it a flick of the finger he listened intently with his ear close to the hub.

"A beautiful ball-bearing race," he remarked, "it runs like silk." Next he turned his attention to the body. "Grand piece of timber, Leslie—though a trifle on the heavy side. It'll take plenty of pulling up a brew."

"I can pull it," said Leslie, stiffening.

"You might find it a shade *front-heavy,*" went on Spit, "which means it'll be hard on the steering unless you keep it well oiled."

"It's well made," said Leslie. "Eh, Spit?"

Spit nodded. "Aye, all the bolts are counter-sunk," he said, "everything chamfered and fluted off to perfection. But—"

"But what?" asked Leslie.

"Do you want me to tell you?" asked Spit.

"Yes, I do," answered Leslie.

"Well, it's got none of *you* in it," said Spit.

"How do you mean?" says Leslie.

"Well, you haven't so much as given it a single tap with a hammer," said Spit. "That trolley will be a stranger to you to your dying day."

"How come," said Leslie, "since I *own* it?"

Spit shook his head. "You don't own it," he said, in a quiet, solemn tone. "You own nothing in this world except those things you have taken a hand in the making of, or else you've earned the money to buy them."

Leslie sat down on *The British Queen* to think this one out. We all sat round, scratching our heads.

"You've forgotten to mention one thing," said Ernie Haddock to Spit, "what about the *speed*?"

"Going down a steep hill," said Spit, "she should hold the road well—an' with wheels like that she should certainly be able to shift some."

"Think she could beat *Egdam*?" ventured Ernie.

"That," said Spit, "remains to be seen."

Ernie gave a shout: "A challenge race! *The British Queen* versus *Egdam*!"

"Not tonight," said Leslie. "I haven't got the proper feel of her yet."

"What about Sunday morning?" I said.

Spit nodded. "As good a time as any."

Leslie agreed. "By then," he said in a challenging tone, "I'll be able to handle her."

Chattering like monkeys, eating bread, carrots, fruit, and bits of toffee, the entire gang of us made our way along the silent Sunday-morning streets for the big race at Cemetery Brew. We were split into two fairly equal sides.

Leslie, in his serge Sunday suit, walked ahead, with Ernie Haddock pulling *The British Queen,* and a bunch of supporters around. They were optimistic, for Leslie had easily outpaced every other trolley during the week, though as yet he had not run against Spit.

Spit was in the middle of the group behind, and I was pulling *Egdam* and keeping the pace easy, for I wanted Spit to keep fresh. He walked in and out among us with an air of imperturbability that, considering the occasion, seemed almost godlike. It inspired a fanatical confidence in us. It was such that Chick Dale, a curly-headed kid with soft skin like a girl's and a nervous lisp, climbed up onto the spiked railings of the cemetery, and, reaching out with his thin fingers, snatched a yellow rose. He ran in front of Spit and thrust it into a small hole in his jersey.

"I pwesent you with the wose of the winner!" he exclaimed.

"And I've a good mind to present you with a clout on the lug," replied Spit, "for pinching a flower from a cemetery. An' what's more, it's bad luck." Seeing Chick's face, he relented. "On second thoughts, Chick, I'll wear it. Ee, wot a 'eavenly smell!"

Happily we went along, and Spit turned to a couple of lads at the back. "Hy, stop that whistling. Don't forget what day it is—folk want their sleep out."

A faint sweated glow had come over Spit's face when we reached the top of the hill, but he was as majestically calm as ever. Taking the bottle of cold water from his trolley seat, he put it to his lips and rinsed out his mouth in the manner of a boxer.

The two contestants were called together by Ernie.

"No bumpin' or borin'," he said.

They nodded.

"The winner," he said, "is the first who puts the nose of his trolley past the cemetery gates."

They nodded.

"Now, who," he asked, "is to be judge?"

Leslie looked at me. "I've no objection to Bill," he said. "I know he's straight."

I hadn't realized I was, I thought, but by heck I will be!

"Ernie here," said Spit, "can be starter."

With that Leslie and Spit shook hands.

"Fly down to them gates," said Ernie to me. He had his father's pigeon-timing watch in his hand. "I'll be setting 'em off dead on the stroke of ten o'clock."

I hurried down to the gates. I looked back and saw the supporters lining themselves on either side of the road.

Leslie was sitting upright on *The British Queen.* Spit was settling himself to ride belly-down. Ernie Haddock, handkerchief raised in the right hand, eye gazing down on the watch in the left, was counting them off—just like when he tossed one of his father's pigeons.

"Five—four—three—two—one—*Off!*"

Spit was away like a shot. That vigorous toe push sent him clean ahead of Leslie. A volley of shouts went up from his supporters, and groans from Leslie's. I saw Spit move straight to the middle of the road camber. Then I ran ahead to take up my position at the winning-post.

When I turned again I was surprised to see that Spit had not increased the lead. In fact, it seemed that Leslie had begun to gain on him. He had settled himself into a crouched position, and those perfect wheels combined with his extra weight were bringing him up with Spit. Not that it seemed possible he could ever catch him. For Spit, lying flat on his trolley, moving with a fine balance, gliding, as it were, over the rough patches, looked to me as though he were a bird that might suddenly open out its wings and fly clean into the air.

The runners along the side could no longer keep up with the trolleys. And now, as they skimmed past the halfway mark and came to the very steepest part, there was no doubt that Leslie was gaining. Spit had never ridden better; he coaxed *Egdam* over the tricky parts, swayed with her, gave her her head, and guided her. Yet Leslie, clinging grimly to the steering-rope of *The British Queen* and riding the rougher part of the road, was actually drawing level. Those beautiful ball-bearing wheels, engineer-made, encased in oil, were holding the road and bringing Leslie along faster than spirit and skill could carry Spit.

Dead level they sped into the final stretch. Spit's slight figure was poised fearlessly on his trolley, drawing the extremes of speed from her. Thundering beside him, anxious but determined, came Leslie. He was actually drawing ahead—and forcing his way to the top of the camber. On they came like two charioteers—Spit delicately edging to the side, to gain inches by the extra downward momentum. I kept my eyes fastened clean across the road as they came belting past the winning-post.

First past was the plate *The British Queen.* I saw that first. Then I saw the heavy rear wheel jog over a pothole and strike Spit's front wheel—sending him in a swerve across the road. Suddenly then, from nowhere, a charabanc came speeding round the wide bend.

Spit was straight in its path. Nothing could avoid the collision. I gave a cry of fear as I saw the heavy solid tyre of the front wheel hit the trolley. Spit was flung up and his back hit the radiator. Then the driver stopped dead.

I got there first. Spit was lying on the macadam road on his side. His face was white and dusty, and coming out between his lips and trickling down his chin was a rivulet of fresh red blood. Scattered all about him were yellow rose petals.

"Not my fault," I heard the driver shouting. "I didn't have a chance. He came straight at me."

The next thing we were surrounded by women who had got out of the charabanc. And then Leslie and all the lads came up.

"Somebody send for an ambulance!" called a woman.

"I'll run an' tell the gatekeeper to telephone," said Ernie Haddock.

"I hadn't a chance," the driver explained to the women.

"A piece of his jersey on the starting-handle there . . ." said someone.

"Don't move him," said the driver to a stout woman who had bent over Spit. "Wait for the ambulance."

"Hush up," she said. She knelt and put a silk scarf under Spit's head. Then she wiped his mouth with her little handkerchief.

He opened his eyes. Glazed they were, as though he couldn't see. A short cough came out of him, then he looked at me and his lips moved.

"Who won?"

"Thee!" blurted out Leslie. "Tha just licked me. Eh, Bill?"

"Aye," I said, "old *Egdam* just pipped *The British Queen.*"

Spit's eyes closed again. The women looked at each other. They nearly all had tears in their eyes. Then Spit looked up again, and his wise, knowing look came over his face. After a minute he spoke in a sharp whisper:

"Liars. I can remember seeing Leslie's back wheel hit my front 'un. I didn't win—I lost." He stared upward for a few seconds, then his eyes twitched and shut.

The driver kept repeating how it wasn't his fault, and next thing the ambulance came. Nearly all the women were crying now, and I saw the look that went between the two men who put Spit on a stretcher—but I couldn't believe he was dead. I had to go into the ambulance with the attendant to give him particulars. I went up the step and sat down inside and looked out the little window as the driver slammed the doors. I saw the driver holding Leslie as a witness. Chick Dale was lifting the smashed-up *Egdam* onto the body of *The British Queen.* People with bunches of flowers in their hands stared after us as we drove off. Then I heard the ambulance man asking me Spit's name. Then he touched me on the elbow with his pencil and said:

"Where *did* he live?"

I knew then. That word "did" struck right into me. But for a minute I couldn't answer. I had to think hard, for the way he said it made it suddenly seem as though Spit Nolan had been dead and gone for ages.

THE QUEEN'S CARE

Elizabeth Jamison Hodges

Long ago when the first of the rulers named Vahram sat upon the ancient throne of Persia, noblemen in that country took great pride in their skill with bow and arrow. The king even maintained a large wilderness where wild boars, lions, and deer were allowed to roam widely that he might hunt them at his pleasure.

One day in his capital at Bishapur, an important wedding was celebrated with high solemnity and great rejoicing. The groom was none other than the ruler's namesake, his oldest son, and the bride a princess with many names, including Mirud, and so was she called.

Now the young prince was enchanted with his wife. She had ten lengthy braids of dark shining hair, a fine aquiline nose, and eyes as bright as precious stones in sunlight. Not only was she fair, but she possessed a voice so remarkable that the music of her singing was sweeter than the song of birds. Moreover, she was tall, strong enough to ride a horse, and able to shoot an arrow like a man.

But Mirud used her marksmanship only as a game. She had no heart for killing real beasts with shiny and frightened eyes. Indeed, unbeknownst to her husband, often at dusk, she slipped away from the palace to bring a little food, tidbits from her own table, to small birds and animals in the hunting park.

After some time there came a day when a handsome son was born to the royal couple. The prince was ecstatic with happiness and hurried to see his wife.

"Whatever boon you ask shall be yours if I am able to provide it," he said. "So reveal to me, pray, the wish of your heart."

"Your Royal Highness is very kind," Mirud said. "I ask only this: that some day when Your Highness becomes king you will have my likeness and that of our son appear with yours on the coins of Persia."

Now because the time when he would succeed his father seemed many morrows away, and because he wished to please his wife at once, the prince promised to do as she had asked. This made Mirud very happy, and she tried her best to keep her husband content and merry too.

Whenever he was ill, she sent all the servants away and with her own hands placed a cool damp cloth on his forehead. If the day was warm, she would fan him, and whenever his spirits were low, she could raise them up by her singing.

Time, however, flows faster than a stream high in the Zagros Mountains, and a year came when the king died. His son ascended the throne as Vahram II. Then he was not only king of Persia but ruler to some degree over other lands far beyond its borders, and sometimes he was even called an emperor. The Mobad, chief of priests of all the temples of fire, invested the new ruler with his diadem of office. It was not long afterwards that Mirud reminded her husband of his promise.

She said, "When new coins are made in this land, Your Majesty, I pray you remember, Sir, along with your own likeness to have that of our son and mine, too, represented upon them. I believe this will please both men and women and bring you, Sir, the love and respect of all your people."

Like a shadow entering a sunlit garden, a frown appeared on the king's brow. Indeed, darkness seemed to spread across his entire face.

"I could not believe you were serious when you spoke of this before," he said, "so neither was I. Never have I known such a thing to be done. If a woman's face were to appear on our coins, we would be laughed at wherever they go, as they are passed from hand to hand in their journeys throughout the world."

The queen said, "I cannot believe, Sir, that you will refuse me this, the only favor I have ever asked of my husband, especially since its execution would be so greatly to Your Majesty's advantage."

"This is a serious matter," Vahram said, a crafty tone creeping into his voice, "but I shall grant your wish only if you can show yourself as skillful as I in a competition with bow and arrow."

Somewhat to his astonishment, Mirud agreed. So the king arranged a test.

One night in early spring, he led her into the great hall of the palace at Bishapur. Here were high walls decorated in yellow, red, and black, and patterns of leafy scrolls. Huge torches illumined a colorful floor with mosaic designs of handsome courtiers and fair ladies.

At one end of this vast room, Mirud saw a small silver bowl. Its base, she was told, had been firmly wedged into the wooden surface of the table whereon it stood.

"Now, let us see," Vahram said, "which of us can shoot most surely toward the center of that vessel."

Then, standing at the opposite end of the great hall and holding in his hand three arrows of a brownish color, Vahram ordered the flames of the torches quenched. In darkness like the depths of a mountain cave, he drew his bow and shot three times.

As each of his arrows struck the target, there was a loud metallic ring. Now, the king thought, my queen will surely withdraw from a test of skills so unequal.

But Mirud accepted her turn. Standing in the same place her husband had stood, she also rapidly loosed three arrows. Everyone present heard the first strike against the bowl. It gave forth the same sort of metallic ring they had heard before. But there was no such sound from her second shot nor from her third.

King Vahram was delighted. He decided the last two had missed, and that now he would be free of his promise. So joyfully, he ordered the torches be relighted.

This done, he saw that his brown arrows had indeed made three separate dents in the small bowl. But the first of Mirud's, which were green in color, had hit the center of it. Her second arrow had stuck in the first and her third had pierced the second in the same way.

When Vahram perceived his marksmanship had not only been equaled but surpassed by the queen's, his surprise was like that of a lion awakened from sleep by a sudden sound of pursuers. Moreover, he was sorely embarrassed, for his courtiers had seen Mirud win the test and now were saying to the queen, "Wonderful! Your Majesty, wonderful!" Besides, he still could not bear the thought of a woman's likeness appearing with his on the coins of the land.

Therefore, he left the hall in a dark fury, which mounted as time passed. Finally, when the queen reminded him of his promise, he grew so enraged that he ordered the poor woman banished forever from his palace and, unarmed, cast out into the wilderness.

There, fierce boars and other wild beasts of the country crouched by day and prowled by night.

Alone in the royal hunting park, the queen hid in a

thicket of tamarisk trees. She expected to be attacked any moment by hungry animals.

After a while, however, it seemed as if they remembered how often she had brought food there to small creatures. The big beasts left her in peace, and the little birds, flying from bush to bush, showed her where wild grapes and white mulberries grew.

So Mirud did not starve, but with many sighs and tears, she wandered for two nights and a day. Then, her clothes badly torn by pushing through rough underbrush, she reached a clearing. Here she lay down to rest in a shady place.

Like the calm surface of a lake reflecting still clouds on a day when the winds are resting, her sleep was peaceful until she was suddenly awakened by a strange chatter. Opening her eyes, Mirud saw close beside her a large and noisy ape. She had never seen such a creature before, and, thoroughly alarmed, screamed with fright.

The ape belonged to a farmer who was working nearby. When he heard a woman's cries of terror, he hurried into the clearing. By the time he reached Mirud, she was nearly hysterical with fear.

"Do not be afraid," the farmer said. "This animal will not harm you. Perhaps instead he can amuse you with his tricks."

When the queen realized she was not in danger from the ape, she asked the farmer about its history.

"He is a chimpanzee and comes from Africa. I call him 'Kim,'" the farmer said. "Once he belonged to a sailor who, finding the animal clever at imitation, taught him a great many tricks. But in the end, the creature was much too clever."

"And how was that?" Mirud asked.

"He was chided by his master," the farmer said, "and decided to even the score. So one day at sea he ran off with a bag of coins belonging to the sailor. Climbing to the top of the mast, the wily beast threw the money, piece by piece, into the ocean. Thus he disposed of all his master's savings.

"The sailor then decided to give him away to whoever would take him. A few months ago, I happened to be on the coast, saw the chimpanzee and heard his story. Coins come to my hand too rarely for worry, and I thought I would like the ape to amuse my family and friends. This I told the sailor, who gave his troublesome animal to me. So both of us were satisfied."

Then the farmer asked the young queen where she lived, and Mirud replied she no longer had a home. When the farmer heard this, and saw that her clothes were ragged and badly soiled, he invited her to his own small house.

His wife gave her a place to sleep, and the couple, not knowing who she was, shared their simple food with the stranger. Indeed, they took care of her as if she had been their daughter. For her part, Mirud tried to help the farmer's wife with the tasks of her home. Though unused to hard work, the queen was so clever with her hands and tried so sincerely to please, that the couple were happy to have her with them.

Meanwhile, as the days passed, King Vahram became exceedingly uneasy. He missed his kind and beautiful wife and ordered a search to find her. When this failed, he grew more and more angry with himself.

As his unhappiness increased, he felt very weary and yet he hardly slept at all. Finally, it was clear that he was seriously ill, and this news spread quickly through the country.

Before long it reached the queen. She guessed that her husband was distressed because he regretted his hasty action towards her.

So she spoke to the farmer and said, "If you would like to help the king recover his health, I believe I can show you how you may do so."

"I?" said the astonished man.

"Go, pray, to His Majesty's court," Mirud said, "and tell those you see that if nobody has yet found a cure for the king's illness, you believe you can make him well."

"But what remedy could I employ?" the farmer said.

The queen answered, "Since his illness stems from unhappiness, you must bring him some pleasure and delight. This you can do with the help of your clever ape." And in detail she explained the matter to him.

So the farmer set out for the palace and told the courtiers he met that he felt sure he could cure the king. At this, they were first amazed, then amused, and finally spent with laughter.

"If the royal doctors cannot succeed," they said, "how can you?"

Indeed, the farmer's offer seemed so absurd that one of the courtiers told the king about it as a joke. When the ruler had listened, however, he ordered the courtier to bring the farmer to him.

"All of our best doctors have failed to cure me," he said to the farmer, "so you might as well tell me what you suggest."

The farmer, who had never been so near the king before, felt his heart tremble, then his hands and legs, but he was eager to help. So he bowed very low and spoke up bravely.

"Sir," he said. "Three things, I believe, are needed: moderation, rest, and cheer. By way of moderation, I humbly suggest the eating of very little. For rest I respectfully advise that Your Majesty have built a small cottage in a quiet valley where nectarine, cherry, and pear trees grow. There, Sir, you may rest away from the throngs of people and distractions of the court. Finally, if permitted, I would wait upon you, Sir, myself, and bring Kim, my clever ape, to cheer and amuse Your Majesty with his tricks and curious antics."

Since all other remedies had failed, the king decided to follow the farmer's advice. Immediately he ordered a new cottage to be built in a fair valley where he might lodge for a time away from the whirl and business of the court. Here too, he would eat but sparingly, enjoying fresh fruit from the trees and listening to the songs of birds, and the farmer would come to care for him and bring his amusing animal.

One day while the cottage was being built, the queen called the ape to her. She let him see her take a cloth and dampen it with cool water from a jug. Then lying down on a bed, she pressed it to her brow. Next, she picked up a fan and began gently to fan herself, and afterwards she sang a little song.

Apes are very imitative creatures. This one was also clever. He watched the queen with great interest.

Finally, Mirud lay down again upon her bed. Right away, copying what he had observed earlier, Kim moistened a piece of cloth with cool water and pressed it on the queen's forehead. Next, he fanned her very gently, and then in a squeaky chatter, made funny noises as if he were trying to sing. At this Mirud laughed aloud and gave him a fresh apricot.

Before long, on a day in summer, the king's new house was completed. By now, he was so ill that he had to be carried into it and placed upon his bed. This stood near a window through which he could see nectarine, cherry, and pear trees growing beside a lake.

Seated on the branches or flying between them were sleek ravens, swift hawks, and a number of waterfowl. Sometimes, too, a lammergeyer, the royal bird, would fly overhead, as if caring and watchful for the king's safety. So agreeable were these sights, that Vahram's health began to improve just a little.

After he had settled in the small house, the farmer brought his ape to amuse the king. Hardly had this creature arrived when he dipped a piece of fine cloth, given to him by the queen, into a jug of cool water and placed it as a compress on the forehead of the ailing ruler.

"Ah," Vahram said to the farmer, "the queen who is gone used to do that for me."

Next Kim picked up a fan, and after running about with it for a few moments, began gently to fan the king.

"You are very kind," Vahram said to the ape. "My dear wife used to do this for me too."

Finally, Kim opened his mouth, and from it issued such a strange conglomeration of sounds that the king could not keep from laughing.

"What a very, very remarkable ape you have!" he said to the farmer. "I truly believe he has been trying to sing for me. My lost love, the queen, used to cheer me with songs when I was ill, but her voice was as sweet as moonlight. How I wish that I had not been so unkind to her and that she were here with me now!"

When the farmer went home that night, he told his wife and Mirud what had happened. The queen's heart filled with joy and seemed to dance like tulips on a windy day.

"Tomorrow," she said to the farmer, "let me go with you. Perhaps I can help take care of His Majesty."

"I am sorry to refuse your request," the man said, "but, except for the servant who stays with the king at night and myself, no persons are allowed to enter the royal cottage. I dare not take you with me."

On the next day, however, as the farmer started out, the queen followed him in secret. When he neared the house where the king was staying, she saw the man stop by a stream to fill a jug with water. While his back was turned, Mirud was able to slip unnoticed into the cottage. Straightly, she went to her husband and fell on her knees beside his couch. With her face hidden, she asked permission to help take care of him.

Vahram at first did not know who was speaking, for he believed his wife had perished long before. But the woman's voice was familiar, and so he bade her rise that he might see her face. When she did so, he was transported with joy to find his own wife and begged her forgiveness. This, she assured him, had long been his.

Then the heart of the king grew as light as an aspen leaf floating through an autumn sky.

"O! my dearest, my love," he said. "What unexpected joy is mine! I thought I should never again see your fair, fair face."

Later, the queen told him all that had happened to her. King Vahram listened and was enthralled while she spoke of the kindness of the farmer and his wife. He also enjoyed the history of the clever ape that had tricked a sailor but amused a king.

Mirud stayed with Vahram and took care of him. Soon he was well, and the royal couple returned to the palace together. There they were welcomed with joy by their son and all the nobles of the court.

After that the emperor in gratitude gave a large tract of land to the farmer, who became a dihqan, the head man of his village.

From then on Vahram kept his temper under guard and, without the queen mentioning the matter again, arranged to have her likeness and that of the prince, their son, appear with his own on the coins of Persia.

Instead of making fun of these portraits, both men and women were happy to see them. So the royal couple lived in peace and high content for many years.

Lucky Boy

Philippa Pearce

This was just about a perfect summer afternoon, with sunshine, flowers blooming, and birds singing, even to a cuckoo (only that happened to be Lucy next door, who was good at it); and it was Saturday into the bargain. Everything was in Pat's favour: jobs done, and his family safely in the back garden. He strolled down the front garden to the front gate. Clicked open the gate . . .

Free . . .

And then: "Where are you going, Pat? Will you take me with you, Pat? Take me too, Pat!" The cuckoo had stopped calling, because Lucy had given up mimicry to poke her face between the slats of the dividing fence. "Take me."

If he went through the gate and on, without her, Lucy would bawl. That was understood on both sides. The question was: Would anyone from either house come in response to the bawling? And if they did, would they bother to get to the bottom of things: detain Pat for questioning, cross-examine him on his plans, ruin his perfect afternoon?

Of course, he could run for it—now, instantly. That was perhaps the only certain way of keeping his afternoon to himself. He would just leave Lucy bawling behind him. What made him hesitate was that once he used to take Lucy on expeditions even without her asking. When Lucy had been a baby in a pram, he had helped to wheel her. Later on, when she was old enough to walk, he had taken her to the sweetshop, and he had even shared his pocket money with her. Not so very long ago he had taken her regularly to the swings and the sandpit and seesaw on the Recreation Ground.

So he paused, holding the gate open before him, to reason with her. "I'm not going where I could take you," he said, "you're too little."

But she simply repeated: "Take me."

Pat had delayed, and Lucy's mother must have been watching from the window. She opened the front door and came down the path towards them, carrying a pair of red sandals. She had misunderstood the situation. "Lucy," she said, "you put your sandals on if you're going out of this garden." And then, to Pat, "Are you taking her to the shops or to the swings?"

Pat was going to neither, so he said nothing.

Lucy's mother went straight on: "Because if it's the shops, she can have fourpence."

"No," said Pat. "Not the shops."

"Well, then!" said Lucy's mother to Lucy. "You do as Pat tells you, now." She turned briskly back to the house. Lucy's mother was always like that.

Lucy had been putting on her sandals. Now she went through her front gate, and waited for Pat to come through his. She held out her hand, and he took it.

They walked to the Recreation Ground, towards the swings. The sun still shone, flowers bloomed, birds sang—and Lucy with them; but the afternoon was ruined for Pat.

They were within sight of the swings. "Will you push me high?" Lucy was saying.

He made up his mind then. Instead of loosening his hold of her hand, so that she could run ahead to the swings, he tightened it. He gripped her attention. "Listen, Lucy. We could go somewhere much better than the swings." Yes, he'd take Lucy, rather than not go at all. "We'll go somewhere really exciting—but secret, Lucy, mind. Just you and me, secretly."

"Secretly?"

"Come on."

They veered abruptly from the direction of the swings and scudded along the fencing that bounded the Recreation Ground on its far side. They left behind them the swingers, the sandpit-players, and even the football-kickers. Down to the lonely end of the Recreation Ground, where Pat had poked about a good deal recently. He had poked about and found a loose fencing stake that could be pried up and swung aside, to make a gap.

"No one's looking. Through here, Lucy—quickly. Squeeze."

Gaps in the fencing of the Recreation Ground were not unheard of; nor boys getting through them when they should not. But trespassing through such holes was disappointing. On the other side of this fence lay only a private garden. True, it ran down to the river; but what was the use of a riverbank neatly turfed and herbaceous-bordered and within spying-distance of its house? And if one tried to go further along the riverbank, one soon came to another fence, and beyond it, another private garden, and so on. Trespassing boys looked longingly over to the other side of the river, which was open country—thin pasturage, often flooded in winter, with ragged banks grown here and there with willow and alder. They looked, and then they turned back through the gap by which they had come. And in due course the groundsman would notice the hole and stop it up.

Pat's hole had not yet been found by the groundsman, which was a bit of luck; but beyond it, in the garden, lay—yes, *lay* was the very word—the best luck of all.

"Now," Pat said, as Lucy emerged from the hole in the fence into the garden. "Keep down behind the bushes, because of being seen from the house, and follow me. This way to the riverbank; and now—look!"

Lucy gazed, bewildered, awed. The turf of the bank had been mutilated and the flower border smashed by a tangle of boughs and twigs that only yesterday had been the crown of an alder tree, high as a house, that grew on the opposite bank. For years the river had been washing away at the roots of the alder, dislodging a crumb of earth here and a crumb there, and in flood time sweeping away the looser projections of its bank. For years the alder had known that its time was coming; no roots could hold out against it. In the drowsy middle of the day, on Friday, there had been no wind, no extra water down the river; but the alder's time had come. It slid a little, toppled a little, and then fell—fell right across the river, bridging it from side to side.

The people of the house were exceedingly annoyed at the damage done to their grass and flowers. They spent the rest of Friday ringing up the farmer from whose land the alder had fallen, but the farmer wasn't going to do anything about a fallen tree until after the weekend; and *they* certainly did not intend to, they said.

They did not know about Pat. After school on Friday, he found his hole in the fence and, beyond it, the new tree bridge to take him across to the far bank of the river.

Then, he had had no time to explore; now, he had.

"Come on!" he told Lucy, and she followed, trusting him as she always did. They forced a passage through the outer branches to the main trunk. The going was heavy and painful. Pat, because he was just ahead of Lucy, shielded her from the worst of the poking, whipping, barring branches; but still he heard from behind him little gasps of hurt or alarm. More complaint than that she would not make.

They got footholds and handholds on the main trunk, and now Pat began—still slowly and painfully—to work his way along it to the far bank. The last scramble was through the tree roots, upended at the base of the trunk, like a plate on its edge. From there he dropped onto the riverbank of that unknown, long-desired country.

And now he looked back for Lucy. She had not been able to keep up with him and was still struggling along the tree trunk, over the middle of the river. She really was too little for this kind of battling—too young; yet Pat knew she would never admit that, never consent to his leaving her behind.

As he watched her creeping along above the water, he was struck by the remembrance that Lucy could not swim. But she was not going to fall, so that did not matter. Here she was at the base of the trunk now, climbing through the tree roots, standing beside him at last. Her face, dirtied and grazed, smiled with delight. "I liked that," she said. She put her hand in his again.

They began to move along the riverbank, going upstream. "Upstream is towards the source of the river," said Pat. "We might find it. Downstream is towards the sea."

"But I'd like to go to the seaside," said Lucy, halting. "Let's go to the seaside."

"No, Lucy. You don't understand. We couldn't possibly. It's much too far." He pulled her again in the upstream direction.

A ginger-coloured, puppyish dog had been watching them from one of the gardens on the other side. They noticed him now. He stared and stared at them, then gave a bark. Before Pat could prevent her, Lucy had barked back—rather well and very provocatively.

"Hush!" said Pat; but he was too late, and Lucy barked again. The dog had cocked his head doubtfully at Lucy's first bark; at the second, he made up his mind. He began to bark shrilly and continuously and as if he would never stop. He pranced along his section of the bank, shrieking at them as they went.

"Now look what you've done!" Pat said crossly. "Somebody will hear and guess something's up."

Lucy began to cry.

"Oh, I didn't mean it," said Pat. "No one's come yet. Stop it, do, Lucy. Please."

She stopped, changing instantly from crying to the happiest smiling. Pat ground his teeth.

The dog continued barking, but soon he could keep level with them no longer, for a garden fence stopped him. He ran up and down the length of it, trying to get through, banging his body against it. He became demented as he saw Lucy and Pat going from him, curving away with the riverbank beyond all possible reach. They heard his barking long after they had lost sight of him.

And now the nettles began. At first only a few, but at the first sting Lucy made a fuss. Then the clumps grew larger and closer together. They might have tried skirting them altogether, by moving in an arc from the riverbank; but in that direction they would have been stopped by another stream, flowing parallel to their own, and not much narrower. They could see that very soon the nettles were filling all the space between the two streams.

Pat considered. He had foreseen the possibility of nettles that afternoon, and was wearing a long-sleeved sweater as well as jeans and socks and sandals. Lucy and Lucy's mother, of course, had foreseen nothing: Lucy was wearing a short-sleeved dress, and her legs were bare. Legs always suffered most among nettles, so Pat took off his sweater and made Lucy put it on like a pair of curiously constructed trousers, with her legs thrust through the sleeves. Then he found himself a stick and began beating a way for them both through the nettle banks.

Whack! and *whack!* left and right, he slashed the nettle stems close to the ground, so that they toppled on either side and before him. Then he trampled them right down, first to one side, then to the other. Then again *whack! whack!* and trample, trample. From behind him Lucy called: "I'd like to do that."

"Oh, I daresay!" he said scornfully.

"Aren't you coming back for me?" she asked next, for his beaten path had taken him almost out of sight. So he went back to her and took her pick-a-back for some way; then decided that didn't help much, and was too tiring anyway. He put her down, and she waited behind him while he whacked. She kept her sleeved legs close together and hugged her bare arms close round her, against the nettles.

The nettles were always there—*whack! whack!* and trample, trample—until suddenly they stopped. There was an overflow channel from the river, manmade of brick and stone and cement patchings; it was spanned by a rather unnecessary bridge with a willow weeping over it. Lucy settled at once on the bridge under the willow to serve tea with leaves for plates and cups, and scrapings of moss for sandwiches, fancy cakes, and jellies. She was very happy. Pat took off his sandals and socks and trod about in the thin film of water that slid from the upper river down the overflow channel into the lower stream. He climbed about on the stone stairs down which the overflow water ran, spattering and spraying, to its new, lower level. The wateriness of it all delighted him.

Then the barking began again. There, on the other side of the river, stood the gingery dog. By what violence or cunning he had got there, it was impossible to say. It was certain, however, that he would bark at them as long as he could see them. Some loose stones were lying in the overflow and Pat picked up several and threw them at the dog. Those that did not fall short, flew wide. The dog barked steadily. Lucy left her tea party and descended onto a slimy stone to see what was happening, and the sliminess of the stone betrayed her: she slipped and sat down in the inch of water that flowed to the lower stream, and began to cry. Pat was annoyed by her crying and because she had sat down wearing—and wetting—

his sweater, and above all because of the ceaseless barking on the other bank.

He hauled Lucy to her feet: "Come *on*!"

Beyond the overflow there were fewer nettles, so that they went faster; but the gingery dog still kept pace with them, barking. But Pat could see something ahead that the dog could not: a tributary that joined the main river on the dog's side and that would check him, perhaps, more effectively than any garden fence. They drew level with the tributary stream; they passed it; and now they were leaving the gingery dog behind, as well as the nettles.

They entered a plantation of willows, low-lying and neglected. Saplings had been planted here long ago for the making of cricket bats; then something had gone wrong, or perhaps the trees had been forgotten. Cricket was still played and willow bats used for it; but these particular willows, full-grown and aging, had never been felled for the purpose. So, in time, like the alder downstream, many of them had felled themselves. Ivy, which had made the plantation its own, had crept up the growing trees and shrouded the fallen ones with loose-hanging swathes of gloomy green.

Lucy was charmed with the place and would have liked to resume the tea party interrupted under the weeping willow. Here were tree stumps for tables, and—an improvement on the overflow—meadowsweet and figwort on the riverbank that could be picked for table decoration. But she would not be left behind if Pat were going on.

Pat saw his chance. "I won't leave you behind," he promised, "but you can play while I just have a look ahead at the way we must go. Then I'll be back for you." Lucy accepted that. He left her choosing a tea table.

So, for a very little while, the afternoon became as Pat had planned it: just for himself. He went on through the sad plantation and came to the end of it—a barbed wire fence beneath which it would not be too difficult to pass. Beyond lay more rough pasture. Far to the right he saw the occasional sun-flash of cars on a distant road. But he was interested only in the river. Looking, he caught his breath anxiously, for a punt was drifting downstream. The only occupant, however, was a man who had shipped his pole in order to drift and doze in the sun; his eyes were shut, his mouth open. He would not disturb Pat and Lucy, if they did not disturb *him*.

Shading his eyes against the sun, Pat looked beyond the punt, as far as he could see upstream. The river appeared very little narrower than at the fallen alder, so probably he was still far from its source. Still the riverbank tempted him. He could see it curving away, upstream and out of sight. Even then he could mark the course of the river by the willows that grew along it. In the distance he could see the top of a building that seemed to be standing on the river; perhaps a mill of some kind, or the remains of one; perhaps a house . . .

Anyway, he would soon see for himself.

He had actually stooped to the barbed wire fencing when he remembered Lucy. Recollecting her, he had also to admit to himself a sound coming from where he had left her, and that had been going on for some time: a dog's furious barking. He sighed and turned back.

Back through the sad plantation to the part of the riverbank where he had left Lucy. "Lucy!" he called; and then he saw the dog on the opposite bank. Its gingeriness was darkened by the water and mud it had gone through in order to arrive where it was. For a wonder, it had stopped barking by the time Pat saw it. It sat there staring at Pat.

"Lucy!" Pat called, and looked round for her. There on a tree stump were her leaf plates, with crumbs of bark and heads of flowers; but no Lucy.

His eyes searched among the trees of the plantation, and he called repeatedly: "Lucy! Lucy! Lucy!"

There was no answer. Even the dog on the opposite bank sat silent, cocking its head at Pat's calling, as if puzzled.

It was not like Lucy to wander from where he had left her. He looked round for any sign of her beside the tea table. He noticed where she had picked meadowsweet and figwort; stems were freshly broken. A wasp was on the figwort. Lucy was afraid of wasps, but perhaps the wasp had not been there when she had picked what she wanted. The figwort with the wasp on it leaned right over the water.

"Lucy!" Pat called again. He went on calling her name while he slowly swivelled round, scrutinizing each part of the willow plantation as he faced it. He came full circle, and was facing the river again.

The river flowed softly, slowly, but it was deep and dark. Every so often, perhaps at distances of many years, somebody drowned in it. Pat knew that.

He looked over the river to the dog and wondered how long he had been there, and why he had barked so furiously, and then stopped.

He looked at the bank where the figwort grew: it was crumbly, and now he noticed that some of it had been freshly broken away, slipping into the water.

He saw the flowing of the water, its depth and darkness. Speechless and motionless he stood there, staring.

The summer afternoon was still perfect, with sunshine, flowers blooming, birds singing, even to the cuckoo. . . .

Then suddenly: *the cuckoo*! He swung round, almost lost his balance on the edge of the riverbank, and, with a shout of "Lucy!" started off in quite the wrong direction. Then he saw a hand that lifted a curtain of ivy hanging over a fallen tree trunk. He plunged towards it and found her. She was hiding in a green ivy cave, laughing at him. He pulled her out, into the open, and began smacking her bare arms, so that she screamed with pain and astonishment and anger. The dog began barking again. Pat was shouting, "You stupid little girl—stupid—stupid—stupid!"

And then another voice was added to theirs, in a bellow. The punt Pat saw earlier had come downstream as far as the plantation, and the man who had been dozing was now on his feet and shouting: "Stop that row, for God's sake! And you ought to be ashamed of yourself—beating your sister like that! Stop it, or I'll come on land and stop you myself with a vengeance!"

The two children stared, still and silent at once. Then Pat gripped Lucy and began to pull her away from the riverbank and the man and the dog. They blundered through the plantation and reached the barbed wire. They crept under it, and Pat set off again, pulling Lucy after him, across the meadows to the right, towards the distant road.

"We're going home," he said shortly when Lucy, in tears, asked where they were going.

"But why aren't we going back by the riverbank and over the tree? I liked that."

"Because we're not. Because I say so."

When they reached the road, they turned in the direction of home. There was a good way to go, Pat knew, and Lucy was already grizzling steadily. She hated to walk when she had to walk. There was not much chance of anyone they knew stopping to give them a lift and, if anyone did, there would be a lot of questions to be answered.

They passed a bus stop and plodded on. Lucy was crying like a toothache. Pat heard a car coming and it passed them. Later, a lorry, and it passed them. Then there was a heavier sound behind them on the road, and Pat turned: "Lucy, quick! Back—run back!"

"Back?"

But Pat was already dragging her with him back to the bus stop, signalling as he ran. The bus drew up for them and they climbed in and sat down. Pat was trembling. Lucy, who had needed a handkerchief for some time now, passed from sobbing to sniffing.

The conductor was standing over them. "Well?" he said.

Pat started. "Two halves to Barley," he said.

The conductor held out his hand.

Pat felt through all the contents of his trouser pockets, but before he reached the bottoms he knew, he remembered: "I've no money."

The conductor reached up and twanged the bell of the bus and the driver slowed to a halt, although there was no bus stop. "I've a heart of gold," said the conductor, "but I've met this trick before on a Saturday afternoon."

Pat could feel the other passengers on the bus were listening intently. Their faces, all turned in his direction, were so many pale blurs to him; almost certainly he was going to cry.

The conductor said, "You've some hard luck story, no doubt, you and your little sister."

"She's not my sister."

A voice from somewhere in the bus—the voice of Mrs. Bovey, who lived down their road—said, "I know him. He's Pat Woods. I'll pay the fare. But what his mother would say . . ."

"You're a lucky boy, aren't you?" the conductor said.

Pat did not look at Mrs. Bovey; he did not thank her; he hated her.

The conductor took Mrs. Bovey's money and twanged the bell again, so that the bus moved on. He held out two tickets to Pat, but did not yet let him take them. "Latest fashion, I suppose?" he said. Pat did not know what he meant until he pointed, and then Pat realized that Lucy was still wearing his sweater as trousers.

"Take that off," Pat ordered Lucy. As she was slow, he began to drag the sweater off her.

The conductor interrupted to hand him the tickets. "You be gentle with your sister," he warned Pat; and from somewhere in the bus a passenger tutted.

"She's not my sister, I tell you."

"No," said Mrs. Bovey, "and what *her* mother will say I don't like to think."

"You'll grant you're in charge of her this afternoon?" said the conductor. "Speak up, boy."

In the silence, Lucy said: "You're making him cry. I hate you. Of course he looks after me. I'm always safe with him."

Pat had turned his head away from them—from all of them—as the tears ran down his cheeks.

THE SECRET OF THE HATTIFATTENERS

Tove Jansson

Once upon a time, rather long ago, it so happened that Moominpappa went away from home without the least explanation and without even himself understanding why he had to go.

Moominmamma said afterwards that he had seemed odd for quite a time, but probably he hadn't been odder than usual. That was just one of those things one thinks up afterwards when one's bewildered and sad and wants the comfort of an explanation.

No one was quite certain of the moment Moominpappa had left.

Snufkin said that he had intended to row out with the hemulen to catch some alburn, but according to the hemulen, Moominpappa had only sat on the veranda as usual and suddenly remarked that the weather was hot and boring and that the landing stage needed a bit of repair. In any case Moominpappa hadn't repaired it, because it was as lopsided as before. Also the boat was still there.

So Moominpappa had set out on foot, and as he could have chosen several directions there was no point in looking for him.

"He'll be back in due time," Moominmamma said. "That's what he used to tell me from the beginning, and he always came back, so I suppose he'll return this time too."

No one felt worried, and that was a good thing. They had decided never to feel worried about each other; in this way everybody was helped to a good conscience and as much freedom as possible.

So Moominmamma started some new knitting without making any fuss, and somewhere to the west Moominpappa was wandering along with a dim idea firmly in his head.

It had to do with a cape he once had seen on one of the family picnics. The cape had pointed straight out to sea, the sky had been yellow, and a bit of wind had

sprung up towards night. He had never been able to go out there to see what was on the other side. The family wanted to turn home for tea. They always wanted to go home at the wrong time. But Moominpappa had stood on the beach for a while, looking out over the water. And at that very moment a row of small white boats with sprit sails had come into sight under land, putting straight out to sea.

"That's hattifatteners," the hemulen had said, and in those words everything was expressed. A little slightingly, a little cautiously, and quite clearly with repudiation. Those were the outsiders, half-dangerous, different.

And then an overpowering longing and melancholy had gripped Moominpappa, and the only thing he knew for certain was that he didn't want any tea on the veranda. Not that evening, nor any other evening.

This had been quite a time ago, but the picture never left him. And so one afternoon he went away.

The day was hot, and he walked at random.

He didn't dare to think about it, nor to feel anything, he simply went on walking towards the sunset, screwing up his eyes under the hatbrim and whistling to himself, but no special tune. There were uphills and downhills, the trees came wandering towards and past him, and their shadows were beginning to lengthen.

At the moment when the sun dipped down into the sea Moominpappa came out onto the long gravel shore where no ways ever stopped and no one ever thought of going for a picnic.

He hadn't seen it before; it was a gray and dreary beach that told him nothing except that land ended and sea started here. Moominpappa stepped down to the water and looked outward.

And naturally—what else could indeed have happened?—at that very moment a little white boat came slowly gliding before the wind along the shore.

"Here they are," Moominpappa said calmly and started to wave.

There were only three hattifatteners aboard the boat. They were quite as white as the boat and the sail. One was sitting at the helm and two with their backs to the mast. All three were staring out to sea and looking as if they had been quarreling. But Moominpappa had heard that hattifatteners never quarrel, they are very silent and interested only in traveling onwards, as far as possible. All the way to the horizon, or to the world's end, which is probably the same thing. Or so people said. It was also said that a hattifattener cared for nothing but himself, and further, that they all became electric in a thunderstorm. Also that they were dangerous company to all who lived in drawing rooms and verandas and were used to doing certain things at certain times.

All this had greatly interested Moominpappa for as long as he could remember, but as it isn't considered quite nice to talk about hattifatteners, except indirectly, he still didn't know whether all those things were true.

Now he felt a shiver from head to tail and in great excitement saw the boat draw nearer. The hattifatteners did not signal to him in reply—one couldn't even imagine them making such large and everyday gestures—but it was quite clear that they were coming for him. With a faint rustling their boat plowed into the gravel and lay still.

The hattifatteners turned their round, pale eyes to Moominpappa. He tipped his hat and started to explain. While he spoke the hattifatteners' paws started to wave about in time to his words, and this made Moominpappa perplexed. He suddenly found himself hopelessly tangled up in a long sentence about horizons, verandas, freedom, and drinking tea when one doesn't want any tea. At last he stopped in embarrassment, and the hattifatteners' paws stopped also.

Why don't they say anything? Moominpappa thought nervously. Can't they hear me, or do they think I'm silly?

He offered his paw and made a friendly, interrogatory noise, but the hattifatteners didn't move. Only their eyes slowly changed color and became yellow as the evening sky.

Moominpappa drew his paw back and made a clumsy bow.

The hattifatteners at once rose and bowed in reply, very solemnly, all three at the same time.

"A pleasure," Moominpappa said.

He made no other effort to explain things, but clambered aboard and thrust off. The sky was burning yellow, exactly as it had been that other time. The boat started on a slow outward tack.

Never in his life had Moominpappa felt so at ease and pleased with everything. He found it splendid for a change not to have to say anything or explain anything, to himself or to others. He could simply sit looking at the horizon, listening to the cluck of the water.

When the coast had disappeared a full moon rose, round and yellow over the sea. Never before had Moominpappa seen such a large and lonely moon. And never before had he grasped that the sea could be as absolute and enormous as he saw it now.

All at once he had a feeling that the only real and convincing things in existence were the moon and the sea and the boat, with the three silent hattifatteners.

And the horizon, of course—the horizon in the distance where splendid adventures and nameless secrets were waiting for him, now that he was free at last.

He decided to become silent and mysterious, like a hattifattener. People respected one if one didn't talk. They believed that one knew a great many things and led a very exciting life.

Moominpappa looked at the hattifatteners at the helm. He felt like saying something chummy, something to show he understood. But then he let it alone. Anyway, he didn't find any words that—well, that would have sounded right.

What was it the Mymble had said about hattifatteners? Last spring, at dinner one day. That they led a wicked life. And Moominmamma had said: That's just talk; but My became enormously interested and wanted to know what it meant. As far as Moominpappa could remember, no one had been really able to describe what people did when they led a wicked life. Probably they behaved wildly and freely in a general way.

Moominmamma had said that she didn't even believe that a wicked life was any fun, but Moominpappa hadn't been quite sure. It's got something to do with electricity, the Mymble had said, cock-surely. And they're able to read people's thoughts, and that's not allowed. Then the talk had turned to other things.

Moominpappa gave the hattifatteners a quick look. They were waving their paws again. Oh, how horrible, he thought. Can it be that they're sitting there reading my thoughts with their paws? And now they're hurt, of course. . . . He tried desperately to smooth out all his thoughts, clear them out of the way, forget all he had ever heard about hattifatteners, but it wasn't easy. At the moment nothing else interested him. If he could only talk to them. It was such a good way to keep one from thinking.

And it was no use to leave the great dangerous thoughts aside and concentrate on the small and friendly sort. Because then the hattifatteners might think that they were mistaken and that he was only an ordinary veranda Moominpappa. . . .

Moominpappa strained his eyes looking out over the sea towards a small black cliff that showed in the moonlight.

He tried to think quite simple thoughts: there's an island in the sea, the moon's directly above it, the moon's swimming in the water—coal-black, yellow, dark blue. At last he calmed down again, and the hattifatteners stopped their waving.

The island was very steep, although small.

Knobbly and dark it rose from the water, not very unlike the head of one of the larger sea serpents.

"Do we land?" Moominpappa asked.

The hattifatteners didn't reply. They stepped ashore with the painter and made fast in a crevice. Without giving him a glance they started to climb up the shore. He could see them sniffing against the wind, and then bowing and waving in some deep conspiracy that left him outside.

"Never mind me," Moominpappa exclaimed in a hurt voice and clambered ashore. "But if I ask you if we're going to land, even if I see that we are, you might still give me a civil answer. Just a word or two, so I feel I've company."

But he said this only under his breath, and strictly to himself.

The cliff was steep and slippery. It was an unfriendly island that told everyone quite clearly to keep out. It had no flowers, no moss, nothing—it just thrust itself out of the water with an angry look.

All at once Moominpappa made a very strange and disagreeable discovery. The island was full of red spiders. They were quite small but innumerable, swarming over the black cliff like a live red carpet.

Not one of them was sitting still; every one was rushing about for all his worth. The whole island seemed to be crawling in the moonlight.

It made Moominpappa feel quite weak.

He lifted his legs, he quickly rescued his tail and shook it thoroughly, he stared about him for a single spot empty of red spiders, but there was none.

"I don't want to tread on you," Moominpappa mumbled. "Dear me, why didn't I remain in the boat. . . . They're too many, it's unnatural to be so many of the same kind . . . all of them exactly alike."

He looked helplessly for the hattifatteners and caught sight of their silhouettes against the moon, high up on the cliff. One of them had found something. Moominpappa couldn't see what it was.

No difference to him, anyway. He went back to the boat, shaking his paws like a cat. Some of the spiders had crawled onto him, and he thought it very unpleasant.

They soon found the painter also and started to crawl along it in a thin red procession, and from there further along the gunwale.

Moominpappa seated himself as far astern as possible.

This is something one dreams, he thought. And then one awakens with a jerk to tell Moominmamma, "You can't imagine how horrible, dearest, such a lot of spiders, you never . . ."

And she awakens too and replies, "Oh, poor Pappa—that was a dream, there aren't any spiders here. . . ."

The hattifatteners were slowly returning.

Immediately every spider jumped high with fright, turned, and ran back ashore along the painter.

The hattifatteners came aboard and pushed off. The boat glided out from the black shadow of the island, into the moonlight.

"Glory be that you're back," Moominpappa cried with great relief. "As a matter of fact, I've never liked spiders that are too small to talk with. Did you find anything interesting?"

The hattifatteners gave him a long moon-yellow look and remained silent.

"I said did you find anything," Moominpappa repeated, a little red in the snout. "If it's a secret of course you can keep it to yourselves. But at least tell me there *was* something."

The hattifatteners were quite still and silent, only looking at him. At this Moominpappa felt his head grow hot and cried, "Do you like spiders? Do you like them or not? I want to know at once!"

In the long ensuing silence one of the hattifatteners took a step forward and spread its paws. Perhaps it had replied something—or else it was just a whisper from the wind.

"I'm sorry," Moominpappa said uncertainly, "I see." He felt that the hattifattener had explained to him that they had no special attitude to spiders. Or else it had deplored something that could not be helped. Perhaps the sad fact that a hattifattener and a Moominpappa will never be able to tell each other anything. Perhaps it was disappointed in Moominpappa and thought him rather childish. He sighed and gave them a downcast look. Now he could see what they had found. It was a small scroll of birch bark, of the sort the sea likes to curl up and throw ashore. Nothing else. You can unroll them like documents: inside they're white and silksmooth, and as soon as they're released they curl shut again. Exactly like a small fist clasped about a secret. Moominmamma used to keep one around the handle of her tea kettle.

Probably this scroll contained some important message or other. But Moominpappa wasn't really curious any longer. He was a little cold, and curled up on the floor of the boat for a nap. The hattifatteners never felt any cold, only electricity.

And they never slept.

Moominpappa awoke by dawn. He felt stiff in the back and still rather cold. From under his hatbrim he could see part of the gunwale and a gray triangle of sea falling and rising and falling again. He was feeling a little sick, and not at all like an adventurous Moomin.

One of the hattifatteners was sitting on the nearest thwart, and he observed it surreptitiously. Now its eyes were gray. The paws were very finely cut. They were flexing slowly, like the wings of a sitting moth. Perhaps the hattifattener was talking to its fellows, or just thinking. Its head was round and quite neckless. Most of all he resembles a long white sock, Moominpappa thought. A little frayed at the lower, open end, and as if made of white foam rubber.

Now he was feeling a little sicker still. He remembered his behavior of last night. And those spiders. It was the first time he had seen a spider frightened.

"Dear, dear," Moominpappa mumbled. He was about to sit up, but then he caught sight of the birch bark scroll and stiffened. He pricked his ears under the hat. The scroll lay in the bailer on the floor, slowly rolling with the movement of the boat.

Moominpappa forgot all about seasickness. His paw cautiously crept out. He gave the hattifatteners a quick look and saw that their eyes as usual were fixed on the horizon. Now he had the scroll, he closed his paw around it, he pulled it towards him. At that moment he felt a slight electric shock, no stronger than from a flashlight battery when you feel it with your tongue. But he hadn't been prepared for it.

He lay still for a long time, calming himself, then started slowly to unroll the secret document. It turned out to be ordinary white birch bark. No treasure map. No code letter. Nothing.

Perhaps it was just a kind of visiting card, politely left on every lone island by every hattifattener to be found by other hattifatteners? Perhaps that little electric shock gave them the same friendly and sociable feeling one gets from a nice letter? Or perhaps they had an invisible writing unknown to ordinary trolls? Moominpappa disappointedly let the birch bark curl itself back into a scroll again, and looked up.

The hattifatteners were regarding him calmly. Moominpappa reddened.

"We're all in the same boat, anyway," he said. And without expecting any reply he spread his paws like he had seen the hattifatteners do, in a helpless and regretful gesture, and sighed.

To this the wind replied with a faint howl in the tight stays. The sea was rolling gray waves all the way to the world's end and Moominpappa thought with some sadness: If this is a wicked life I'd rather eat my hat.

There are many kinds of islands, but all those that are small enough and far enough are without exception rather sad and lonesome. The winds chase all around them, the yellow moon increases and wanes again, the sea becomes coal-black every night, but the islands are always unchanged, and only hattifatteners visit them now and then. They are not even real islands. They are skerries, rocks, reefs, forgotten streaks of land that perhaps even sink under water before daybreak and rise over the surface again during the night to take a look around. One can't know.

The hattifatteners visited them all. Sometimes a birch bark scroll was there waiting for them. Sometimes there was nothing; the islet was just a smooth seal's back surrounded by breakers, or a ragged rock with high banks of red seaweed. But on the summit of every island the hattifatteners left behind them a small white scroll.

They have an idea, Moominpappa thought. Something that's more important to them than all other matters. And I'm going to follow them about until I know what it is.

They met no more red spiders, but Moominpappa remained aboard every time they landed. Because those islands made him think of other islands far behind him, the picnic islands, the green and leafy bathing inlets, the tent, and the butter container cooling in the shadow by the boat, the juice glasses in the sand, and the bathing trunks adry on a sun-hot boulder. . . . Not that he missed that kind of secure veranda life for a minute. Those were just thoughts that came flapping past and made him a bit sad. Thoughts about small and insignificant things.

As a matter of fact Moominpappa had started to think in a wholly new manner. Less and less often he mused about things he had encountered in his kindly and checkered life, and quite as seldom did he dream about what his future would bring him.

His thoughts glided along like the boat; without memories or dreams, they were like gray wandering waves that didn't even want to reach the horizon.

Moominpappa stopped trying to talk to the hattifatteners. He sat staring seawards, just as they did; his eyes had turned pale like theirs, taking the color of the sky. And when new islands swam into view he didn't even move, only tapped his tail once or twice against the floor.

Once, as they glided along on the back of a slow, tired swell, Moominpappa fleetingly thought: I wonder if I'm beginning to resemble a hattifattener.

It had been a very hot day, and towards evening a mist rolled in from the sea. It was a heavy, curiously reddish mist. Moominpappa thought it looked menacing and a little alive.

The sea serpents were snorting and wallowing far out; he could catch a glimpse of them at times. A round, dark head, startled eyes staring at the hattifatteners, then a splash from a tail fin and a quick flight back into the mist.

They're afraid like the spiders were, Moominpappa thought. Everyone's afraid of hattifatteners. . . .

A far-away thunderclap went rolling through the silence, and everything was quiet and immobile once more.

Moominpappa always had thought thunderstorms very exciting. Now he didn't have any opinion about them. He was quite free, but he just didn't seem to have any likings anymore.

At that moment a strange boat steered out of the mist with a large company aboard. Moominpappa jumped to his feet. In a moment he had become the old Moominpappa again, waving his hat about and shouting. The strange boat was coming straight towards them. It was white, the sail was white. And the people aboard it were white. . . .

"Oh, I see," Moominpappa said. He sat down again. The two boats continued their courses without exchanging any greeting.

And then one boat after the other glided out of the dark mist, all going the same way and all manned by hattifatteners. Sometimes by seven, sometimes by five, or eleven, at times even by one solitary hattifattener, but always by an odd number.

The mist cleared away and rolled into the slightly reddish evening dusk. The sea seemed to be packed with boats. All were on their way towards a new island, a low skerry with no trees and no high cliffs.

The thunder went rolling over again. It was hiding somewhere in the enormous black cloud that was now climbing higher and higher over the horizon.

One boat after the other put in and lowered sail. The lonely beach was already thronged by hattifatteners that had arrived earlier and were standing bowing to each other.

As far as one could see, white solemn beings were walking about and exchanging bows to right and left. They emitted a faint rustling sound and were constantly waving their paws. The beach grass whispered around them.

Moominpappa was standing aside by himself. He tried desperately to find his own hattifatteners among the crowd. He felt it to be important. They were the only ones he knew . . . slightly. Very slightly. But still.

They had disappeared in the throng; he could see no differences in the many hundreds of hattifatteners, and all at once Moominpappa was caught by the same terror as on the spider island. He pulled his hat down to his eyebrows and tried to look tough and at ease at the same time.

His hat was the only fixed and absolute thing on this strange island where all was white and whispering and vague.

Moominpappa didn't quite trust himself any longer, but he believed in his hat; it was black and resolute, and inside it Moominmamma had painted the words "M.P. from your M.M." to distinguish it from all other high hats in the world.

Now the last boat had landed and been pulled ashore, and the hattifatteners stopped rustling. They turned their reddish eyes towards Moominpappa, all together, and the next instant they began to move in his direction.

They want a fight, Moominpappa thought and was suddenly wide awake and rather elated. In that moment he felt like fighting anyone just to fight and shout and feel sure that everyone else was wrong and deserving a good hiding.

Only hattifatteners never fight, nor do they object to anything or dislike anyone or hold any opinion at all.

They came to exchange bows with Moominpappa, all the hundreds of them, and Moominpappa tipped his hat and bowed in reply until he felt a headache coming on. Hundreds of paws waved at him until he also began waving his from sheer exhaustion.

When the last hattifattener had passed him Moominpappa had forgotten all about wanting a fight. His mind was polite and smooth, and he followed the others, hat in hand, through the whispering grass.

The thunderstorm had climbed high in the meantime and was hovering in the sky like a wall about to fall down. High up a wind was blowing, driving small rugged tufts of cloud before it in scared flight.

Close to the sea sudden and fitful lightning was flashing, switching off and flaring up again.

The hattifatteners had assembled in the center of the island. They had turned southwards, where the thunderstorm waited, exactly like seabirds before a gale. One after the other they began to light up like little lamp bulbs, flaring in time with the lightning. The grass around them was crackling with electricity.

Moominpappa had laid himself on his back and was staring up at the pale green leaves around him. Light, delicate leaves against a dark sky. In his easy chair at home he had a cushion embroidered with fern leaves by Moominmamma. Pale green leaves against black felt. It was very beautiful.

The thunderstorm was nearing rapidly. Moominpappa felt faint shocks in his paws and sat up. There was rain in the air.

All of a sudden the hattifatteners began fluttering their paws like moth wings. They were all swaying, bowing, and dancing, and a thin, gnat-like song arose from the lonely island. It was the howl of the hattifatteners, a lonely and yearning sound like wind in a bottleneck. Moominpappa felt an irresistible desire to do as the hattifatteners did. To sway back and forth, to sway and howl and rustle.

He felt a prickle in his ears and his paws began to wave. He rose to his feet and started to walk towards the hattifatteners. Their secret's got to do with thunderstorms, he thought. It's thunderstorms they are always looking for and longing for. . . .

Darkness fell over the island, and the lightning flashes were running straight down from the sky like streams of dangerously white and hissing liquid. Far out the wind started to roar and then the thunder broke loose, the fiercest thunder Moominpappa had ever experienced.

Heavy wagons of stone were rolling and rumbling back and forth, to and fro, and the wind caught hold of Moominpappa and threw him back in the grass.

He sat holding his hat and feeling the wind blow through him, and all of a sudden he thought: No. What's come over me? I'm no hattifattener, I'm Moominpappa. . . . What am I doing here?

He looked at the hattifatteners and with electric simplicity he understood it all. He grasped that only a great thunderstorm could put some life in hattifatteners. They were heavily charged but hopelessly locked up.

They didn't feel, they didn't think—they could only seek. Only in the presence of electricity they were able to live at last, strongly and with great and intense feelings.

That was what they longed for. Perhaps they were even able to attract a thunderstorm when they assembled in large crowds. . . .

Yes, that must be the solution, Moominpappa thought. Poor hattifatteners. And I was sitting on my veranda believing they were so remarkable and free, just because they never spoke a word and were always on the move. They hadn't a single word to say and nowhere to go. . . .

The skies opened and the rain crashed down, gleaming white in the flashes of lightning.

Moominpappa jumped to his feet. His eyes were as blue as ever, and he shouted:

"I'm going home! I'm leaving at once!"

He stuck his snout in the air and pulled his hat securely over his ears. Then he ran down to the beach, jumped aboard one of the white boats, hoisted sail, and put straight out to the stormy sea.

He was himself once again, he had his own thoughts about things, and he longed to be home.

Just think, never to be glad nor disappointed, Moominpappa mused while the boat was carried along in the gale. Never to like anyone and get cross at him and forgive him. Never to sleep or feel cold, never to make a mistake and have a belly ache and be cured from it, never to have a birthday party, drink beer, and have a bad conscience. . . .

How terrible.

He felt happy and drenched and not in the least afraid of the thunderstorm. At home they would never have electric light, he decided; they'd keep the old kerosene lamps.

Moominpappa longed for his family and his veranda. All of a sudden he thought that at home he could be just as free and adventurous as a real pappa should be.

THE HAPPY PRINCE

Oscar Wilde

High above the city, on a tall column, stood the statue of the Happy Prince. He was gilded all over with thin leaves of fine gold, for eyes he had two bright sapphires, and a large red ruby glowed on his sword hilt.

He was very much admired indeed. "He is as beautiful as a weathercock," remarked one of the Town Councillors, who wished to gain a reputation for having artistic tastes. "Only not quite so useful," he added, fearing lest people should think him unpractical, which he really was not.

"Why can't you be like the Happy Prince?" asked a sensible mother of her little boy, who was crying for the moon. "The Happy Prince never dreams of crying for anything."

"I am glad there is someone in the world who is quite happy," muttered a disappointed man as he gazed at the wonderful statue.

"He looks just like an angel," said the Charity Children as they came out of the cathedral in their bright scarlet cloaks and their clean white pinafores.

"How do you know?" said the Mathematical Master. "You have never seen one."

"Ah! but we have, in our dreams," answered the children; and the Mathematical Master frowned and looked very severe, for he did not approve of children dreaming.

One night there flew over the city a little Swallow. His friends had gone away to Egypt six weeks before, but he had stayed behind, for he was in love with the most beautiful Reed. He had met her early in the spring as he was flying down the river after a big yellow moth, and had been so attracted by her slender waist that he had stopped to talk to her.

"Shall I love you?" said the Swallow, who liked to come to the point at once, and the Reed made him a low bow. So he flew round and round her, touching the water with his wings, and making silver ripples. This was his courtship, and it lasted all through the summer.

"It is a ridiculous attachment," twittered the other Swallows. "She has no money, and far too many relations." And indeed the river was quite full of Reeds. Then, when the autumn came they all flew away.

After they had gone he felt lonely and began to tire of his lady-love. "She has no conversation," he said, "and I am afraid that she is a coquette, for she is always flirting with the wind." And certainly, whenever the wind blew, the Reed made the most graceful curtsies. "I admit that she is domestic," he continued, "but I love travelling, and my wife, consequently, should love travelling also."

"Will you come away with me?" he said finally to her, but the Reed shook her head, she was so attached to her home.

"You have been trifling with me," he cried. "I am off to the Pyramids. Goodbye!" and he flew away.

All day long he flew, and at nighttime he arrived at the city. "Where shall I put up?" he said. "I hope the town has made preparations."

Then he saw the statue on the tall column.

"I will put up there," he cried. "It is a fine position, with plenty of fresh air." So he alighted just between the feet of the Happy Prince.

"I have a golden bedroom," he said softly to himself as he looked round, and he prepared to go to sleep; but just as he was putting his head under his wing a large drop of water fell on him. "What a curious thing!" he cried. "There is not a single cloud in the sky, the stars are quite clear and bright, and yet it is raining. The climate in the north of Europe is really dreadful. The Reed used to like the rain, but that was merely her selfishness."

Then another drop fell.

"What is the use of a statue if it cannot keep the rain off?" he said. "I must look for a good chimney pot." And he determined to fly away.

But before he had opened his wings, a third drop fell, and he looked up, and saw—Ah! what did he see?

The eyes of the Happy Prince were filled with tears, and tears were running down his golden cheeks. His face was so beautiful in the moonlight that the little Swallow was filled with pity.

"Who are you?" he said.

"I am the Happy Prince."

"Why are you weeping then?" asked the Swallow. "You have quite drenched me."

"When I was alive and had a human heart," answered the statue, "I did not know what tears were, for I lived in the Palace of Sans-Souci, where sorrow is not allowed to enter. In the daytime I played with my companions in the garden, and in the evening I led the dance in the Great Hall. Round the garden ran a very lofty wall, but I never cared to ask what lay beyond it, everything about me was so beautiful. My courtiers called me the Happy Prince, and happy indeed I was, if pleasure be happiness. So I lived, and so I died. And now that I am dead they have set me up here so high that I can see all the ugliness and all the misery of my city, and though my heart is made of lead yet I cannot choose but weep."

"What! is he not solid gold?" said the Swallow to himself. He was too polite to make any personal remarks out loud.

"Far away," continued the statue in a low musical voice, "far away in a little street there is a poor house. One of the windows is open, and through it I can see a woman seated at a table. Her face is thin and worn, and she has coarse, red hands, all pricked by the needle, for she is a seamstress. She is embroidering passionflowers on a satin gown for the loveliest of the Queen's maids of honour to wear at the next Court ball. In a bed in the corner of the room her little boy is lying ill. He has a fever, and is asking for oranges. His mother has nothing to give him but river water, so he is crying. Swallow, Swallow, little Swallow, will you not bring her the ruby out of my sword hilt? My feet are fastened to this pedestal and I cannot move."

"I am waited for in Egypt," said the Swallow. "My friends are flying up and down the Nile and talking to the large lotus flowers. Soon they will go to sleep in the tomb of the great King. The King is there himself in his painted coffin. He is wrapped in yellow linen and embalmed with spices. Round his neck is a chain of pale green jade, and his hands are like withered leaves."

"Swallow, Swallow, little Swallow," said the Prince, "will you not stay with me for one night and be my messenger? The boy is so thirsty and the mother so sad."

"I don't think I like boys," answered the Swallow. "Last summer, when I was staying on the river, there were two rude boys, the miller's sons, who were always throwing stones at me. They never hit me, of course. We swallows fly far too well for that, and besides I come of a family famous for its agility; but still, it was a mark of disrespect."

But the Happy Prince looked so sad that the little Swallow was sorry. "It is very cold here," he said, "but I will stay with you for one night and be your messenger."

"Thank you, little Swallow," said the Prince.

So the Swallow picked out the great ruby from the Prince's sword and flew away with it in his beak over the roofs of the town.

He passed by the cathedral tower, where the white marble angels were sculptured. He passed by the palace and heard the sound of dancing. A beautiful girl came out on the balcony with her lover. "How wonderful the stars are," he said to her, "and how wonderful is the power of love!"

"I hope my dress will be ready in time for the State ball," she answered. "I have ordered passionflowers to be embroidered on it, but the seamstresses are so lazy."

He passed over the river and saw the lanterns hanging to the masts of the ships. He passed over the Ghetto and saw the old Jews bargaining with each other, and weighing out money in copper scales. At last he came to the poor house and looked in. The boy was tossing feverishly on his bed, and the mother had fallen asleep, she was so tired. In he hopped, and laid the great ruby on the table beside the woman's thimble. Then he flew gently round the bed, fanning the boy's forehead with his wings. "How cool I feel!" said the boy. "I must be getting better." And he sank into a delicious slumber.

Then the Swallow flew back to the Happy Prince and told him what he had done. "It is curious," he remarked, "but I feel quite warm now, although it is so cold."

"That is because you have done a good action," said the Prince. And the little Swallow began to think, and then he fell asleep. Thinking always made him sleepy.

When day broke he flew down to the river and had a bath. "What a remarkable phenomenon!" said the Professor of Ornithology as he was passing over the bridge. "A swallow in winter!" And he wrote a long letter about it to the local newspaper. Everyone quoted it, it was full of so many words that they could not understand.

"Tonight I go to Egypt," said the Swallow, and he was in high spirits at the prospect. He visited all the public monuments and sat a long time on the top of the church steeple. Wherever he went the Sparrows chirruped and said to each other, "What a distinguished stranger!" So he enjoyed himself very much.

When the moon rose he flew back to the Happy Prince. "Have you any commissions for Egypt?" he cried. "I am just starting."

"Swallow, Swallow, little Swallow," said the Prince, "will you not stay with me one night longer?"

"I am waited for in Egypt," answered the Swallow. "Tomorrow my friends will fly up to the Second Cataract. The river-horse couches there among the bulrushes, and on a great granite throne sits the God Memnon. All night long he watches the stars, and when the morning star shines he utters one cry of joy, and then he is silent. At noon the yellow lions come down to the water's edge to drink. They have eyes like green beryls, and their roar is louder than the roar of the cataract."

"Swallow, Swallow, little Swallow," said the Prince, "far away across the city I see a young man in a garret.

He is leaning over a desk covered with papers, and in a tumbler by his side there is a bunch of withered violets. His hair is brown and crisp, and his lips are red as a pomegranate, and he has large and dreamy eyes. He is trying to finish a play for the Director of the Theatre, but he is too cold to write any more. There is no fire in the grate, and hunger has made him faint."

"I will wait with you one night longer," said the Swallow, who really had a good heart. "Shall I take him another ruby?"

"Alas! I have no ruby now," said the Prince. "My eyes are all that I have left. They are made of rare sapphires, which were brought out of India a thousand years ago. Pluck out one of them and take it to him. He will sell it to the jeweller, and buy firewood, and finish his play."

"Dear Prince," said the Swallow, "I cannot do that." And he began to weep.

"Swallow, Swallow, little Swallow," said the Prince, "do as I command you."

So the Swallow plucked out the Prince's eye and flew away to the student's garret. It was easy enough to get in, as there was a hole in the roof. Through this he darted, and came into the room. The young man had his head buried in his hands, so he did not hear the flutter of the bird's wings, and when he looked up he found the beautiful sapphire lying on the withered violets.

"I am beginning to be appreciated," he cried. "This is from some great admirer. Now I can finish my play." And he looked quite happy.

The next day the Swallow flew down to the harbour. He sat on the mast of a large vessel and watched the sailors hauling big chests out of the hold with ropes. "Heave a-hoy!" they shouted as each chest came up. "I am going to Egypt!" cried the Swallow, but nobody minded, and when the moon rose he flew back to the Happy Prince.

"I am come to bid you goodbye," he cried.

"Swallow, Swallow, little Swallow," said the Prince, "will you not stay with me one night longer?"

"It is winter," answered the Swallow, "and the chill snow will soon be here. In Egypt the sun is warm on the green palm trees, and the crocodiles lie in the mud and look lazily about them. My companions are building a nest in the Temple of Baalbek, and the pink and white doves are watching them and cooing to each other. Dear Prince, I must leave you, but I will never forget you, and next spring I will bring you back two beautiful jewels in place of those you have given away. The ruby shall be redder than a red rose, and the sapphire shall be as blue as the great sea."

"In the square below," said the Happy Prince, "there stands a little match-girl. She has let her matches fall in the gutter, and they are all spoiled. Her father will beat her if she does not bring home some money, and she is crying. She has no shoes or stockings, and her little head is bare. Pluck out my other eye, and give it to her, and her father will not beat her."

"I will stay with you one night longer," said the Swallow, "but I cannot pluck out your eye. You would be quite blind then."

"Swallow, Swallow, little Swallow," said the Prince, "do as I command you."

So he plucked out the Prince's other eye, and darted down with it. He swooped past the match-girl and slipped the jewel into the palm of her hand. "What a lovely bit of glass!" cried the little girl, and she ran home laughing.

Then the Swallow came back to the Prince. "You are blind now," he said, "so I will stay with you always."

"No, little Swallow," said the poor Prince, "you must go away to Egypt."

"I will stay with you always," said the Swallow, and he slept at the Prince's feet.

All the next day he sat on the Prince's shoulder and told him stories of what he had seen in strange lands. He told him of the red ibises, who stand in long rows on the banks of the Nile and catch goldfish in their beaks; of the Sphinx, who is as old as the world itself, and lives in the desert, and knows everything; of the merchants, who walk slowly by the side of their camels and carry amber beads in their hands; of the King of the Mountains of the Moon, who is as black as ebony and worships a large crystal; of the great green snake that sleeps in a palm tree, and has twenty priests to feed it with honey cakes; and of the pygmies who sail over a big lake on large flat leaves and are always at war with the butterflies.

"Dear little Swallow," said the Prince, "you tell me of marvellous things, but more marvellous than anything is the suffering of men and of women. There is no Mystery so great as Misery. Fly over my city, little Swallow, and tell me what you see there."

So the Swallow flew over the great city, and saw the rich making merry in their beautiful houses, while the beggars were sitting at the gates. He flew into dark lanes, and saw the white faces of starving children looking out listlessly at the black streets. Under the archway of a bridge two little boys were lying in one another's arms to try and keep themselves warm. "How hungry we are!" they said. "You must not lie here," shouted the watchman, and they wandered out into the rain.

Then he flew back and told the Prince what he had seen.

"I am covered with fine gold," said the Prince. "You must take it off, leaf by leaf, and give it to my poor; the living always think that gold can make them happy."

Leaf after leaf of the fine gold the Swallow picked off, till the Happy Prince looked quite dull and gray. Leaf after leaf of the fine gold he brought to the poor, and the children's faces grew rosier, and they laughed and played games in the street. "We have bread now!" they cried.

Then the snow came, and after the snow came the frost. The streets looked as if they were made of silver, they were so bright and glistening; long icicles like crystal daggers hung down from the eaves of the houses, everybody went about in furs, and the little boys wore scarlet caps and skated on the ice.

The poor little Swallow grew colder and colder, but he would not leave the Prince, he loved him too well. He picked up crumbs outside the baker's door when the baker was not looking, and tried to keep himself warm by flapping his wings.

But at last he knew that he was going to die. He had just enough strength to fly up to the Prince's shoulder once more. "Goodbye, dear Prince!" he murmured. "Will you let me kiss your hand?"

"I am glad that you are going to Egypt at last, little Swallow," said the Prince. "You have stayed too long here; but you must kiss me on the lips, for I love you."

"It is not to Egypt that I am going," said the Swallow. "I am going to the House of Death. Death is the brother of Sleep, is he not?"

And he kissed the Happy Prince on the lips, and fell down dead at his feet.

At that moment a curious crack sounded inside the statue, as if something had broken. The fact is that the leaden heart had snapped right in two. It certainly was a dreadfully hard frost.

Early the next morning the Mayor was walking in the square below in company with the Town Councillors. As they passed the column he looked up at the statue. "Dear me! How shabby the Happy Prince looks!" he said.

"How shabby, indeed!" cried the Town Councillors, who always agreed with the Mayor, and they went up to look at it.

"The ruby has fallen out of his sword, his eyes are gone, and he is golden no longer," said the Mayor. "In fact, he is little better than a beggar!"

"Little better than a beggar," said the Town Councillors.

"And here is actually a dead bird at his feet!" continued the Mayor. "We must really issue a proclamation that birds are not to be allowed to die here." And the Town Clerk made a note of the suggestion.

So they pulled down the statue of the Happy Prince. "As he is no longer beautiful he is no longer useful," said the Art Professor at the University.

Then they melted the statue in a furnace, and the Mayor held a meeting of the Corporation to decide what was to be done with the metal. "We must have another statue, of course," he said, "and it shall be a statue of myself."

"Of myself," said each of the Town Councillors, and they quarrelled. When I last heard of them they were quarrelling still.

"What a strange thing!" said the overseer of the workmen at the foundry. "This broken lead heart will not melt in the furnace. We must throw it away." So they threw it on a dustheap where the dead Swallow was also lying.

"Bring me the two most precious things in the city," said God to one of His Angels; and the Angel brought Him the leaden heart and the dead bird.

"You have rightly chosen," said God, "for in my garden of Paradise this little bird shall sing for evermore, and in my city of gold the Happy Prince shall praise me."

KADDO'S WALL

West African folktale as told by
Harold Courlander and George Herzog

In the town of Tendella in the Kingdom of Seno, north of the Gulf of Guinea, there was a rich man by the name of Kaddo. His fields spread out on every side of the town. At plowing time hundreds of men and boys hoed up his fields, and then hundreds of women and girls planted his corn seed in the ground for him. His grain bulged in his granary, because each season he harvested far more than he could use. The name of Kaddo was known far and wide throughout the Kingdom of Seno. Travelers who passed through the town carried tales of his wealth far beyond Seno's borders.

One day Kaddo called all of his people in the town of Tendella together for a big meeting in front of his house. They all came, for Kaddo was an important man, and they knew he was going to make an important announcement.

"There's something that bothers me," Kaddo said. "I've been thinking about it for a long time. I've lain awake worrying. I have so much corn in my granary that I don't know what to do with it."

The people listened attentively, and thought about Kaddo's words. Then a man said:

"Some of the people of the town have no corn at all. They are very poor and have nothing. Why don't you give some of your corn to them?"

Kaddo shook his head and said, "No, that isn't a very good idea. It doesn't satisfy me."

Another man said to Kaddo:

"Well, then, you could lend corn to the people who have had a bad harvest and have no seed for the spring planting. That would be very good for the town and would keep poverty away."

"No," Kaddo said, "that's no solution either."

"Well, then, why not sell some of your corn and buy cattle instead?" still another man said.

Kaddo shook his head.

"No, it's not very good advice. It's hard for people to advise a rich man with problems like mine."

Many people made suggestions, but nobody's advice suited Kaddo. He thought for a while, and at last he said:

"Send me as many young girls as you can find. I will have them grind the corn for me."

The people went away. They were angry with Kaddo. But the next day they sent a hundred girls to work for him as he had asked. On a hundred grindstones they began to grind Kaddo's corn into flour. All day long they put corn into the grindstones and took flour out. All day long the people of the town heard the sound of the grinding at Kaddo's house. A pile of corn flour began to grow. For seven days and seven nights the girls ground corn without a pause.

When the last grain of corn was ground into flour, Kaddo called the girls together and said:

"Now bring water from the spring. We shall mix it with the corn flour to make mortar out of it."

So the girls brought water in water pots and mixed it with the flour to make a thick mortar. Then Kaddo ordered them to make bricks out of the mortar.

"When the bricks are dry, then I shall make a wall of them around my house," he said.

Word went out that Kaddo was preparing to build a wall of flour around his house, and the people of the town came to his door and protested.

"You can't do a thing like this, it is against humanity!" they said.

"It's not right, people have no right to build walls with food!" a man said.

"Ah, what is right and what is wrong?" Kaddo said. "My right is different from yours, because I am so very rich. So leave me alone."

"Corn is to eat, so that you may keep alive," another said. "It's not meant to taunt those who are less fortunate."

"When people are hungry it is an affront to shut them out with a wall of flour," another man said.

"Stop your complaints," Kaddo said. "The corn is mine. It is my surplus. I can't eat it all. It comes from my own fields. I am rich. What good is it to be rich if you can't do what you want with your own property?"

The people of the town went away, shaking their heads in anger over Kaddo's madness. The hundred girls continued to make bricks of flour, which they dried in the sun. And when the bricks were dry Kaddo had them begin building the wall around his house. They used wet dough for mortar to hold the bricks together, and slowly the wall grew. They stuck cowry shells into the wall to make beautiful designs, and when at last the wall was done, and the last corn flour used up, Kaddo was very proud. He walked back and forth and looked at his wall. He walked around it. He went in and out of the gate. He was very happy.

And now when people came to see him they had to stand by the gate until he asked them to enter. When the workers who plowed and planted for Kaddo wanted to talk to him, Kaddo sat on the wall by the gate and listened to them and gave them orders. And whenever the people of the town wanted his opinion on an important matter he sat on his wall and gave it to them, while they stood and listened.

Things went on like this for a long time. Kaddo enjoyed his reputation as the richest man for miles around. The story of Kaddo's wall went to the farthest parts of the kingdom.

And then one year there was a bad harvest for Kaddo. There wasn't enough rain to grow the corn, and the earth dried up hard and dusty like the road. There wasn't a single ear of corn in all of Kaddo's fields or the fields of his relatives.

The next year it was the same. Kaddo had no seed corn left, so he sold his cattle and horses to buy corn for food and seed for a new planting. He sowed corn again, but the next harvest time it was the same, and there wasn't a single ear of corn on all his fields.

Year after year Kaddo's crops failed. Some of his relatives died of hunger, and others went away to other parts of the Kingdom of Seno, for they had no more seed corn to plant and they couldn't count on Kaddo's help. Kaddo's workers ran away, because he was unable to feed them. Gradually Kaddo's part of the town became deserted. All that he had left were a young daughter and a mangy donkey.

When his cattle and his money were all gone, Kaddo became very hungry. He scraped away a little bit of the flour wall and ate it. The next day he scraped away more of the flour wall and ate it. The wall got lower and lower. Little by little it disappeared. A day came when the wall was gone, when nothing was left of the elegant structure Kaddo had built around his house, and on which he had used to sit to listen to the people of the town when they came to ask him to lend them a little seed corn.

Then Kaddo realized that if he was to live any longer he must get help from somewhere. He wondered who would help him. Not the people of Tendella, for he had insulted and mistreated them and they would have nothing to do with him. There was only one man he could go to, Sogole, king of the Ganna people, who had the reputation of being very rich and generous.

So Kaddo and his daughter got on the mangy, underfed donkey and rode seven days until they arrived in the land of the Ganna.

Sogole sat before his royal house when Kaddo arrived. He had a soft skin put on the ground next to him for Kaddo to sit upon, and had millet beer brought for the two of them to drink.

"Well, stranger in the land of the Ganna, take a long drink, for you have a long trip behind you if you come from Tendella," Sogole said.

"Thank you, but I can't drink much," Kaddo said.

"Why is that?" Sogole said. "When people are thirsty they drink."

"That is true," Kaddo replied. "But I have been hungry too long, and my stomach is shrunk."

"Well, drink in peace then, because now that you are my guest you won't be hungry. You shall have whatever you need from me."

Kaddo nodded his head solemnly and drank a little of the millet beer.

"And now tell me," Sogole said. "You say you come from the town of Tendella in the Kingdom of Seno?

I've heard many tales of that town. The famine came there and drove out many people, because they had no corn left."

"Yes," Kaddo said. "Hard times drove them out, and the corn was all gone."

"But tell me, there was a rich and powerful man in Tendella named Kaddo, wasn't there? What ever happened to him? Is he still alive?"

"Yes, he is still alive," Kaddo said.

"A fabulous man, this Kaddo," Sogole said. "They say he built a wall of flour around his house out of his surplus crops, and when he talked to his people he sat on the wall by his gate. Is this true?"

"Yes, it is true," Kaddo said sadly.

"Does he still have as many cattle as he used to?" Sogole asked.

"No, they are all gone."

"It is an unhappy thing for a man who owned so much to come to so little," Sogole said. "But doesn't he have many servants and workers still?"

"His workers and servants are all gone," Kaddo said. "Of all his great household he has only one daughter left. The rest went away because there was no money and no food."

Sogole looked melancholy.

"Ah, what is a rich man when his cattle are gone and his servants have left him? But tell me, what happened to the wall of flour that he built around his house?"

"He ate the wall," Kaddo said. "Each day he scraped a little of the flour from the wall, until it was all gone."

"A strange story," Sogole said. "But such is life."

And he thought quietly for a while about the way life goes for people sometimes, and then he asked:

"And were you, by any chance, one of Kaddo's family?"

"Indeed I was one of Kaddo's family. Once I was rich. Once I had more cattle than I could count. Once I had many cornfields. Once I had hundreds of workers cultivating my crops. Once I had a bursting granary. Once I was Kaddo, the great personage of Tendella."

"What! You yourself are Kaddo?"

"Yes, once I was proud and lordly, and now I sit in rags begging for help."

"What can I do for you?" Sogole asked.

"I have nothing left now. Give me some seed corn, so that I can go back and plant my fields again."

"Take what you need," Sogole said. He ordered his servants to bring bags of corn and to load them on Kaddo's donkey. Kaddo thanked him humbly, and he and his daughter started their return trip to Tendella. They traveled for seven days. On the way Kaddo became very hungry. He hadn't seen so much corn for a long time as he was bringing back from the Kingdom of the Ganna. He took a few grains and put them in his mouth and chewed them. Once more he put a few grains in his mouth. Then he put a whole handful in his mouth and swallowed. He couldn't stop. He ate and ate. He forgot that this was the corn with which he had to plant his fields. When he arrived in Tendella he went to his bed to sleep, and when he arose the next morning he ate again. He ate so much of the corn that he became sick. He went to his bed again and cried out in pain, because his stomach had forgotten what to do with food. And before long Kaddo died.

Kaddo's grandchildren and great-grandchildren in the Kingdom of Seno are poor to this day. And to the rich men of the country the common people sometimes say:

"Don't build a wall of flour around your house."

DITA'S STORY

Mary Q. Steele

Ever since she was five years old Dita had wanted to become a witch.

When Dita was five years old her mother lay dying of an unknown fever. Dita's father asked the village priest for help, but the priest refused. The priest said Dita's mother was a wicked woman and deserved to die, for twice he had seen her coming out of sacred places she should never have entered and once she had slapped her mother-in-law.

So Dita's father had taken much meat and many hides and all five of the beautiful river pearls he had found in his lifetime and traveled some distance to another town. He had paid all these things to the witch who lived in that town and she had returned to his house with him.

She had fed Dita's mother on brews and potions. She had spoken many incantations in a low, guttural voice and made curious symbols in the air around the sick woman's bed.

And Dita's mother had recovered.

But more than that, marvelous as it was to Dita, the witch had taken a great interest in Dita, who was small for her age and had a weak and withered arm. The witch had talked to the little girl and showed her some of the strange things she carried in her witch's bundle and let her help in gathering certain herbs and roots.

So Dita made up her mind to become a witch. She told no one.

Three years later her mother was dead, killed by a tree falling on her as she was gathering nuts in the forest. The priest of the village pointed out that she had been a wicked woman and deserved to die.

Dita's father did not marry again but left her in the care of her two sisters, older than she. And though the sisters were good to her, Dita missed her mother.

After some time the sisters married, first one, then the other, and neither of them wished to bring Dita to live with her and her new husband. For she was still small and weak and had a wizened arm and was not much use in a household. Although she was willing and tried very hard, she could not dig in the garden very well or drive the beasts home from pasturing or carry heavy burdens.

She could tend the fire and cook, she could gather nuts and berries and fruits in the forest, but that was almost all. Her older sisters, though they loved her and were kind to her, did not believe their husbands should be asked to provide for one who could give so little in return.

Yet Dita's father was eager that she too should marry and leave home, for he felt that he was growing old and he wished to sit in the square with the other old men and be cared for by his sons-in-law and his nephews.

Dita secretly looked with favor upon one of the young men of the town, a man a little younger than she, who had already proven himself to be a wise man and a good hunter. It was not unusual for women of that village to marry men younger than themselves.

Still he was not yet of an age to marry and take on the care of a wife and family. More than that, he was strong and handsome and many girls besides Dita planned to be his wife.

Dita watched his comings and goings and promised herself that by the time he was old enough to marry she would be stronger and comelier and that she would be his choice. Her father had no such hopes and went about seeking someone to marry his daughter, someone who, for one reason or another, would not be particular or ask too many questions about Dita's skills or abilities.

And after some time he found such a one. A man came to ask permission to marry Dita, an old man who lived alone, far from the village. He was too old to care for his few beasts and his small garden alone. He had no children or close relatives. He did not like living in the town. Thus he wished to marry, now close to the end of his life, and have such help as a wife might offer.

He thought Dita could manage the tasks he would require of her, for they were not great. The two of them could dig the garden and herd the little flock and milk it.

Dita told her father that she did not wish to marry yet and certainly not an old man, who could not hunt and would be dead in a few years.

"The choice is not yours to make," her father told her. "I do not want to force you into marrying this man, but there is no other willing to have you. At least when he dies you will have a house and a garden and some beasts. And he has a distant kinsman who brings him meat on occasion. No doubt the kinsman will feel some obligation to you when the old man dies."

Dita could see that her father was distressed for her. He was in truth growing old and wished to provide for her. It seemed to Dita that there must be some better way.

"Let us wait awhile," she suggested. Perhaps in a while the old man would be dead or find someone else to marry.

Or someone else would want to marry Dita.

"Very well," her father answered. "We will wait two months. But no longer."

He looked gravely at his daughter. "I do not want to die without knowing that my youngest child has some possessions of her own," he said. "Your sisters and their husbands no doubt can help you in good times. But they have families of their own now, and in bad times they must put their families first. In bad times a woman alone, yet who has a house and a garden, can survive, at least."

What he said was true and still Dita did not want to marry the old man. Still she yearned to be the wife of Nogaro, the young man of her choosing. Two months was not a long enough time. It would be longer than that before Nogaro thought of marrying.

So Dita went to the priest.

The old priest, who had thought her mother a wicked woman, was dead. The new priest was a younger man, and tender-hearted. The ills and wickednesses of his people troubled him even more than they troubled those who suffered from them.

Whenever he looked at Dita he trembled for her future. Even more than her father, he worried over what would become of her.

Now he said, as brusquely as he could, for he wished always to hide his pity, "What is it that you want? A woman is ill and needs my attention, so do not bother me with trifles."

Dita was a little afraid, for though she suspected that he was a man who sympathized with her, she could not be sure, for he never spoke to her in any other way.

But what she had come about was no trifle. "Sir," she said quietly, "I wish to become a witch."

The priest stared at her in amazement. No one before had ever said such a thing to him.

Then he said, and now his voice was gentle, "Why would you want such a thing? The life of a priest or witch is hard. And all sorts of dangers lie in wait for them that other people never encounter. One must be very brave and strong to be a witch."

Then Dita was silent in her turn. She did not want to say what her true reasons were. She did not wish to say that she hoped to avoid marrying an old man and that she hoped to learn some charm that would make her a fit wife for Nogaro.

Nor did she want to tell him of the witch who had cured her mother—and how the old priest had disapproved of the witch and of Dita's mother and of the cure. The new priest might not like hearing such things from her, though he must surely remember. All the village had known these things and had talked of them for many days.

At last Dita said, "I am brave. I am not strong, but I am brave. I have long wanted to be a witch and now the time has come."

The priest shook his head.

"We have never had a witch in our town," he pointed out. "I do not think the time has come. I cannot give you the knowledge you must have without a great deal of time and trouble. If I should take such time and trouble and then the village should not accept you, I would be filled with regrets. And so would you."

Dita stood for a while gazing down at the dust under their feet. "But you could do it?" she asked finally. "If you were willing, you would know how?"

"Of course," he answered. "I am a priest. One does not get to be a priest without knowing such things."

Dita went away and in two months she married the old man. Before the marriage she dreamed strange, sorrowful dreams and woke in tears, but there was nothing she could do.

Her sisters comforted her when they saw how she grieved. "We will look after you," they promised.

But the old man lived a long way from the village. Her sisters would seldom see her and they would forget, having worries and troubles of their own.

And the day came and the old man arrived and took her away.

The house was dirty and full of spiders, his beasts were small but ill-tempered, and the garden was neglected and full of stones and weeds.

She chased out the spiders and tidied the house, and that she could do well enough. But she found it hard to manage the beasts, and when they strayed she was seldom able to bring them back and had to wait until they returned of their own accord.

And hoeing and tending the garden tired her very soon, so that she could work in it only an hour or two without sitting to rest for a long time. The old man was impatient with her and prodded her in the ribs when she grew weary and sat down to rest. He pinched her arms when she let the beasts stray.

He complained of the meals, which were bad, not because of Dita's cooking but because the vegetables from the garden were small and tough and flavorless and because the meat the kinsman sometimes brought them was old and half-rotted.

At night the old man made terrible noises in his sleep, blabbering and snoring so that Dita often went out of the house and slept in the open, though she was afraid with the forest too close around her and no other people near.

And at last one day she could bear it no longer. She left and walked back to her village and sought out her father, where he sat in the square with the other old men.

"Let me come home," she pleaded. "I cannot stay with him. Let me come home and I will keep your house and tend your garden till you die, and then I will die too."

Her father was saddened. He had thought she would grow resigned to her life with the old husband.

"I have given you to him," he told her seriously. "Unless he injures you or starves you or ties you to a post, I cannot take you back. Moreover, I have no house and garden now. It belongs to your elder sister and her husband, as is customary. And I sit in the square with the other old men and food is brought to us and we sleep where we will. You must return. A few pinches and prods cannot harm you, and he is too weak to do you any real hurt. In a day or two I will send one of your brothers-in-law to bring you some meat and help you in the garden. But more than that I cannot do."

And he looked at her with sorrow, for she seemed very tired and tears had reddened her eyes, and he thought perhaps he should not have let the old man marry her.

But what else had there been to do?

So when the old man came for her, Dita went back with him. And as they left the town Nogaro passed them and greeted them politely. But Dita did not answer and the old man only grunted, for he was furious that he had had to come again to the village to fetch his wife home.

In a few days Dita's second sister's husband came to their house and brought a young deer which he had killed. He stayed and sharpened the blades of the two hoes and helped Dita plant some new crops. He told the old man he must tether his beasts so that they could not run away from Dita.

Dita was sorry when he left. But the old husband was not sorry. He had not enjoyed having a young man tell him what to do.

When they were alone again, he pinched and prodded Dita more than ever. He laughed when her new crops were all destroyed by insects.

But when one of his beasts died, he did not laugh. He trembled with anger and blamed it on Dita, even though it was clear that the creature had died of old age and its own meanness.

After that each day became worse and worse and she grew wearier and wearier. And so one morning she did not go into the garden or to bring the little beasts out of their pen and take them to the grazing grounds.

Instead she walked into the forest and went on walking. It was quiet and cool, a bird sang somewhere far off, and the odor of fallen leaves and living leaves was sweet.

I will live here, thought Dita. I will live here in peace, for I will not stay any longer with that old man and his pinches and his rages. And I have no place to go, so I will find a hollow tree to sleep in and a spring to drink from. I will eat nuts and fruits and berries and the birds shall be my family and friends.

For she had always loved the songs of birds.

She wandered a long way, but as she did not know where she was going, she traveled almost in a circle and soon found herself close to the place where she had entered the forest.

She heard the old man calling for her and she ran in fear. She ran among the trees and bushes until she could go no farther. She saw a great fruit tree ahead of her and stumbled toward it, thinking she might climb up into its branches and hide.

Instead, when she reached it, the ground beneath her feet suddenly gave way and she fell into a deep sinkhole between two big roots of the fruit tree. Her breath left her body and for a moment all was darkness.

Presently her lungs began to work again and she could see light coming down into the cave from the opening above her. And she thought herself safe. She did not believe the old man could find her here.

She shrank into the farthest corner of the hole and waited. She heard nothing and after a long while she was easy, sure that her husband had gone away, perhaps back to her village to search for her.

She looked about her then. The light was dim but she could see that the hole was not large, though it was very deep. There was a tiny spring at the bottom of one wall and she thought that perhaps at some time the water had gushed forth strongly and made this hollow in the earth.

She could not get out. The walls were far too high, and when she tried to climb them the soil crumbled under her hands and feet. She tried climbing up in many places and each time had to give up.

She was not frightened. When her husband did not find her in her father's village, he would come back to look for her and help her out. And then another time she could run away from him and plan more carefully how she would go and not fall into some hole.

But after some hours, when the day darkened and she knew that night would soon be upon the world, she grew afraid. Would some wild animal jump into the pit and kill her? Once again she cowered in the farthest corner.

The shadows grew deeper until she could see nothing at all. She heard the little spring whispering to itself and in the forest nightbirds called strangely and around her crickets whistled. She sat straining for the sound of paws or the snuffle of wolves, but nothing happened and at last she fell asleep.

When she woke it was daylight and she was terribly hungry. She drank the water of the spring and found a fruit which had fallen from the tree above her. She hoped that more would tumble in, but none did. So she pulled roots from the walls of her prison and chewed these. Surely someone would find her that day.

She waited as patiently as she could. Every now and then she was sure she heard the noise of approaching feet and she jumped up, crying out gladly. Each time she was disappointed and no one came.

And so one day passed and another and another. Once or twice she was certain someone walked by, and she called and called. But the walker either could not hear her or mistook her voice for some curious bird or insect and went by unheeding.

Hunters came this way often—one of them would surely hear her. The old husband would come for her. She would be glad to see even him. But no one came.

Dita was no longer afraid at night, for night and day were misery alike. Why had no one wanted to search for her? Why had everyone left her here in this dreadful place, dank and dim and cold as a grave? Was she to die here in truth?

She grew hungrier and hungrier with nothing to eat but an occasional fruit that dropped through the opening and the few roots she could claw out of the earth and now scarcely had the strength to chew. The nighttime crickets sometimes hopped close to her and she considered eating them, but she did not. It was not that she was repelled by the thought of eating insects, but that she had a certain fellow feeling for these small creatures, held captive here as she was and treated as indifferently by the world.

Why had not her father or her brothers-in-law or even her sisters come seeking her when the old man told them of her absence? Was she so worthless and so little loved? Was there no one to whom she mattered any longer?

She lost count of the days and grew weaker and weaker. And at last she made up her mind that indeed help was not forthcoming and she would die. She lay down on the floor of the pit and plastered her eyes shut with mud, for it was the custom among her people to close the eyes of the dead with earth. She placed her hands at her sides, palms downward, again according to the ways of her people.

And then she waited to die. It was the middle of the day and the birds were silent, and the crickets. Only the tiny spring whispered and whispered and whispered while Dita waited to die. . . .

But in the world above some women from Dita's village had ventured far into the forest gathering fruits and berries. One of them walked toward the great fruit tree through the roots of which Dita had fallen many days before.

The woman saw the gaping hole and wondered about it. Out of curiosity she walked quietly to it and peered into its depths. She could faintly see the body of a dead girl lying at the bottom of the hole, a small thin girl with her eyes covered with earth and her hands palms downward at her sides.

The woman was frightened and backed softly away and then ran to tell the others. "Come look!" she called. "A dead girl is lying yonder at the bottom of a hole."

The others were reluctant to see such a sight. It was not good to look upon the dead, especially one who lay dead in such a strange and unacceptable place.

"Send for the priest," said one of them. "He will know what to do."

And after some talk it was decided that three of the women should go and fetch the priest and the other three stay and watch the pit and its terrible contents.

Dita, lying on the earthen floor, heard nothing of this, only dimly the sound of the little spring, whispering and whispering. So when the priest, a while later, leaned over and saw her and cried out, "It is Dita!" she was too astonished to move.

And not until he had descended to the floor and touched her hand did she find the strength to sit up and scrape the mud from her lids and gaze up at him. The priest gave a great gasp of astonishment and fear and sprang away from her.

Those staring into the pit shouted in horror. "The dead girl is come alive! The dead girl moves!" Several of them ran away and would not look.

In the cave the priest touched Dita's cold arm timorously. "Dita," he said. "Is it you? Are you alive or dead?"

She could not answer. In truth she did not know. She had certainly thought herself dead.

"She cannot speak," the priest called up to the others. "We must lift her out."

So the men the priest had brought with him made a sort of chair of ropes and he raised her to her feet and placed her in it and the others pulled her up.

She could not stand and the full light of day dazzled her and she trembled violently. By and by she recovered herself somewhat, and still she did not speak. Her voice seemed to have left her and words swam through her mind without sense or order. The others stayed well away from her.

Then the men hauled the priest up from the pit. And again he touched her arm and spoke to her. He took some powder from his bundle and sprinkled himself with it, to ward off harm that might come to him from touching and speaking with a dead girl, and he sprinkled a little on Dita. He chanted a prayer to his guardian spirit, and then he felt safe.

He called to the others, "Bring food. For as she has been dead, she will not have eaten for a while, she will be hungry. And if she eats, we will surely know she is alive again."

One of the women came forward unwillingly and gave him some fruit and he in turn offered it to Dita. She took it in her quivering fingers and bit into it and then ate it all.

"You see," the priest exclaimed. "She has been dead and now is alive and eats like any living person!"

Still the others kept their distance.

"You need not fear," the priest told them. "I am here. If this is an evil thing which has happened, I can protect you. The evil will fall upon me and I will know what to do."

The others came closer then and looked at Dita with wondering eyes.

"Her husband's house is nearby," one of them said. "We should take her there and ask him how she came to die. Perhaps he placed her body in the hole instead of bringing her to the village to be buried properly. Perhaps that is why she came alive when the priest touched her. She thought he had come to see that she was buried as she should be."

"That may be so," the priest answered. "We will see."

One of the men picked Dita up and carried her to the old man's house. The priest walked beside him and kept his hand on the man's shoulder so that no ill could come to him from his mysterious burden.

The old husband was tending his garden. "Why have you brought this one here?" he asked angrily. "She ran away into the forest and would not come back. I no longer wish to have her for my wife. She is useless to me."

Dita understood what he said and for the first time in many days she was happy. Her father had not known she was missing and that was why he had not come searching for her. The old man had not considered it worth the trouble to make the long walk to the village to look for her or to tell her family she was gone.

He did not want her for a wife. Never again would he prod her or pinch her or screech at her in his wild way. She almost spoke, to say that she was glad. But still the words would not come to her properly and still she was not sure that she had not died and come back to life.

The priest questioned the old man. Had Dita been alive and well when he last saw her? Did he know anything about her death?

The old man shook his head. "What do you mean? She is not dead. She is there, alive."

The priest saw that he indeed knew nothing.

"You must come back to the village and give her back to her father," the priest said severely. "It was wrong not to come when she first ran into the forest."

They went away then in a long procession, leaving the old husband standing in his weedy garden. The men took turns carrying Dita, though she was no great weight, and the priest walked beside each one who carried her and warded off any danger that might come from this girl who had died and then come alive.

Her father was in the square with the other old men and when he heard what had befallen her, he was amazed.

"How did it come to happen?" he asked, and the priest replied, "We do not know and she cannot tell us. But it is a strange and wonderful thing that has taken place."

"But what will become of her now?" asked her father. "If her husband gives her back to me, alas, I have no place for her. And this is not my daughter Dita any longer. One does not die and come back to life and remain the same person."

"That is likely true," agreed the priest. "And so I will take her to my home and care for her and see what person she has become. Perhaps we will discover how this has come about and then we will know what to do."

And he took Dita home with him.

His wife was not afraid and she fed and bathed this new person. She cried out when she saw how thin and frail the girl was.

"She is nothing but bones!" the priest's wife exclaimed. "She must have been dead many days."

"Perhaps," answered the priest. "But there is no harm in her. I have not felt the presence of any evil. We will care for her and see what happens."

The new person was grateful to be well cared for. She ate and grew strong and though she helped about the house and garden she was not asked to perform tasks beyond her strength. No one pinched or prodded her when she stopped to rest.

In the evenings the people of the village came to see her and talk to her and ask her about the time when she had been dead.

"I do not remember," she told them again and again. "I do not remember anything of when I was dead."

One man walked from another town because he had heard of the wonder and came to tell of another time when it had happened.

"My own grandfather died," he told the priest. "He died in his home and was buried properly. But the next day he sat up in his grave and was alive again. And like this one he could not speak of what had happened to him."

"What did he become?" asked the priest, and the man replied, "Nothing. For in a week he was dead again and this time he did not come back to life. He lay in his grave and rotted with the other dead."

"It may be that will happen with this person," said the priest. "But I think not. For she grows stronger all the time, and speaks often, though she does not remember anything of her life before she died or of the time while she was dead."

And everyone was kind to her and no longer feared her but was glad that this happy thing had occurred, that a young and feeble girl had escaped from the hard cold grasp of death.

Still the priest knew that he could not keep her in his house forever. He must discover as soon as he could what person she had become and what was to be done with her.

So one day he took her by her hand and led her to a quiet place away from the village and spoke to her soberly. "The time has come for us to decide why you have died and come alive again," he told her and she nodded. "We must know what person you have become and what that person is to do."

He looked into her eyes for a long time. "Do you remember being Dita and being married to the old man who lives in the forest?"

After a while she answered honestly, "No." For she had lived with the priest and his wife for many weeks and come to love them deeply and she felt that they loved her. She could no longer bear to think of the wretched days when she had been Dita, whose father had married her to an old husband, or of the prods and pinches the old man had given her and his terrible snore and his vile-tempered little beasts.

And most of all she could not bear to think of the long, hungry days and nights in the dark cave and her sorrow that no one cared enough to look for her and her fear of everything.

She could remember it, a little, if she wanted to and if she tried hard enough, but it all seemed something that had happened to someone else. So she could honestly say "No" to the priest's question.

"Then do you know what person you have become and why this thing has happened to you?" he asked.

And the new person thought for many minutes and finally she replied, "I do not know what person I am now. But this thing has happened to me in order that I may become a witch. That is what I believe."

The priest recalled that Dita too had once said she wished to become a witch.

"Perhaps that is true," he said. "There is much to be done in the town and I am sometimes in need of help. If you became a witch, you could help me. The people here think highly of you. But first I must visit all my sacred places and ask permission of their guardians. They will know if it is to be."

Thus it was decided that the new person had come to be a witch, if it was permitted. Every day the priest visited his holy places and implored their guardians for a sign, whether of pleasure or displeasure. When he came back to his house, he made no mention of these visits to anyone and especially not to the new person.

And she waited patiently and spoke with the people of the village, who treated her with friendliness and respect. They did not know what her plans were or what the priest was doing.

And after some time the priest again took her hand and led her to that quiet place away from the town.

"I have been to my sacred places," he told her, "and all their guardians have sent me messages that you should undergo the training that a witch must undergo. But I warn you that it is a long and wearisome process. You may fail and then I cannot help you."

"What will become of me if I fail?" asked the new person in a whisper.

"I do not know," responded the priest. "Perhaps you will die again. Or perhaps you will become once more only Dita."

It would be the same thing, the new person told herself. For the old husband had died recently and even if he were still alive, he would not want her. She would be without land or possessions and she would not matter to anyone and would likely perish in some time of hunger or drought or other peril.

And the new person was afraid and yet she was willing to try, for it seemed to her to be a witch would be a good thing, as it had seemed to Dita.

Very soon she began to learn the things a witch must know. She learned how to make brews and potions and she learned songs and prayers to chant and the names of holy objects in a special language.

And this was only the beginning. She spent many hours alone in the forest, listening for the voices of the forest spirits and saying over and over the words that would make them happy and pleased with her.

She spent many hours in the village, walking with people and observing all the things they did that would make the spirits look with displeasure upon them, and searching all her own words and acts to see that she was no better than the men and women around her. For the things they did which troubled their invisible guardians, she herself often did too.

And all these deeds were done in secrecy, for the village must not know that the new person was learning to be a witch.

And after some time the priest sent her away into the gray land between living and dying. He took her into the forest and gave her a drink of many ingredients and by and by she went away into the gray land.

At first she saw nothing but grayness, as though a dense fog had fallen over the world. But gradually her sight cleared and things came rushing at her, things she did not know existed and could not afterwards have described to anyone, not even the priest. Shapes and colors of kinds she had never seen before danced before her eyes. And then there was again gray fog, and when it cleared she saw once more the witch woman who had cured her mother, and the banks of the river where her father had found his beautiful river pearls, and the old village priest.

And then she saw Dita being pinched and prodded by the old man and the sight made her want to weep with rage and pity. In the gray land, however, mortals must not move or weep or cry out. They must simply go as a cloud goes with the wind. And she was strong and did not cry out or weep.

She saw the great fruit tree among the roots of which she had fallen into the pit and seeing it frightened her horribly for a reason she could not understand. But she was brave and did not scream.

She drifted on and on, and the things she saw became more and more terrible and fearsome and the effort not to move or cover her eyes made her wearier and wearier, and when she thought she could bear it no longer, must leave and come back to the real world no matter what befell her, the priest touched her hand as he had when she lay dead at the bottom of the sinkhole, and she came out of the gray land and into daylight and warmth and the sound of birdsong.

"You are brave and strong," the priest said. "For I was

with you part of the time, and it was a most terrible ordeal."

And the new person was pleased and smiled at his words, for she knew she had been brave and strong.

And some days later when she was recovered, the priest told her, "Now there is but one thing left to do. It is not difficult, but it is important. If it is not done, you cannot become a witch. And there is nothing you or I can do to make things happen one way or the other. For now you must be claimed by a spirit, who will give you true power. I do not know what that spirit will be and I can have no influence over which spirit chooses you or whether any does. If all the spirits refuse you, then you cannot be a witch."

And the new person trembled, but she followed the priest into the forest and sat where he told her to. And then he went away and she waited.

She waited two days and two nights and part of another day. She was not afraid in the darkness, even though once a wolf walked quite near, for the priest had protected her with a charm and no living thing dared harm her.

But no spirit appeared and that frightened her. Was she to die again after all her long troubles?

And then it happened and she knew a spirit had come to claim her. She saw nothing and heard nothing, only felt a warm presence, good and full of love. She knew what it was. It was the spirit of the great fruit tree among whose roots she had fallen into the pit.

And she heard in her mind a voice, as sweet as early morning birdsong, speaking to her. "She who was once Dita, I claim you for my own and you are now a witch, with all a witch's powers."

And the new person's heart filled with joy. The voice went on. "I know you have deceived the priest, as you know you have, but you did not do it purposely. You have endured a great deal and you have been strong and brave. You have done all things properly and you are fit for the honor that has come to you. But you must remember always to use your powers wisely and for good. And never can you use them on yourself or to further your own aims. You cannot make yourself stronger or more comely or heal your wizened arm. If you do, then you will cease to be a witch and become Dita again."

The new person shuddered as though a cold wind had blown upon her. Some small part of her had known this all along, some small part of her had expected it. But she was not truly prepared for it, and it was as though on a summer day an icy wind had struck her. Nevertheless she said nothing and listened carefully.

"As long as you remember this," said the spirit of the fruit tree, "then you may be a witch and your name will be Halana and you will live in happiness and respect."

And then the presence was gone, but in Halana's hand was a branch of the great fruit tree, with leaves and blossoms and fruit.

She returned to the priest and told him all that the spirit had said to her, except the words about the deception. This, she knew, was something the spirit would want her to tell no one—and Halana herself had been a little surprised when she recognized that it was true. And now that she was Halana, it was no longer true, for Dita was dead and Halana was alive.

There was a celebration in the village to welcome the new witch. And many people brought Halana small gifts and told her they were glad to have a witch among them, for the priest needed help and no boy in the village had come forward to seek the training needed. Nor had any boy been singled out in any way to show that the spirits favored him and wished him for a priest.

So Halana took up her duties as a witch. At first she did small things. She helped find lost objects of little value and protected children against the stings of certain annoying insects.

But soon the priest called on her to do more important things, to help the gardens thrive and cause a spring which had become foul to yield fresh water once again.

She became a person of much importance in the village. Young women came to her for charms to make certain young men look on them with favor and old women came to her for potions to take the ache from their knees and hands. A man whose disposition was so bad that he shouted at his children and threw things at his beasts and made his wife weep asked for Halana's help and she was able to make him better-tempered. She was pleased to be of service.

The work was difficult and often took more strength than she had known she possessed. But Halana always did her best and she was given many things as pay so that it did not matter that she had no possessions of her own. She lived in a small house on the priest's land and was well supplied with food and even owned two mild little beasts that she could easily tend. And she mattered very much to many people.

And still Nogaro had not asked any of the young women of the village to be his wife. Halana watched him now and again as he passed her house and she wondered.

And after some time the priest took her with him when he cared for people who were ill and she aided in the cures. And when, once in a while, the remedies failed, as once in a while they must, with him she was able to comfort those who had been parted from a mother or father, husband or wife or child.

And it seemed to Halana a good and worthwhile thing to be a witch, worth the long years of having been Dita, worth the old husband's pinches and even the long terrible days in the pit, when it had seemed that she was unloved and unwanted. Even when the work was longer and harder than she would have thought it possible to bear, it seemed a good thing.

The priest was pleased with her and her fame grew and sometimes, as her father had fetched the witch from a far village to cure her mother, sometimes from far away men and women came to ask her help or guidance.

And then one day Nogaro's father came to her.

"I hope you keep well," he said.

"I am well," she answered. "And you and your family?"

Nogaro's father looked troubled.

"We are in good health," he said. "But I am concerned about my son Nogaro. He is long past the age to choose a wife and have a family of his own. He is a fine young man and a good hunter and any of the young women of the town would be pleased to marry him. I would like you to provide something that would cause him to look with love upon one of these young women, so that he would want to marry her. I myself would prefer that he marry Manika, daughter of Tadar, for she is a person of many admirable qualities, and healthy and good-looking as well. But I would rather he chose anyone at all than go longer without a wife. My other son has been married for some time and I would wish Nogaro to be as happy."

Halana looked at him gravely.

"It is a difficult task you have asked of me," she said. "I must have time to prepare myself. Come back in two days and I will tell you if it is a thing I can properly do."

Nogaro's father left and Halana sat for a long while. She remembered the day she had become a witch and the icy cold wind that had touched her when the spirit had given its warning. She remembered how she had shuddered.

She got up at last and went into the forest and walked until she came to the old husband's house, falling down now and filled once more with dust and spiders. How miserable Dita had been there! How she had longed to be the wife of some good man, of Nogaro!

She walked away again and came to the foot of the great fruit tree. At the priest's order the hole among the roots had been filled in and marked with a sacred sign. This was the most holy of Halana's three holy places and no one might come here without her permission. She waited now to feel the presence of the tree spirit, but it did not come. And after a while she spoke a few words to invoke the spirit and still nothing happened.

Was there no way? Would the spirit of the tree not help her to be a witch and still become Nogaro's wife? If she used her powers to make Nogaro choose her to wed, then she would no longer be a witch, only Dita, frail and thin and with a withered arm. Nogaro would have married a woman not able to care properly for a garden and beasts and children when he was away hunting.

Nogaro was a good young man. If he loved her truly, he would not care about such things perhaps. But perhaps he would know that she had lost her powers as a witch in order to make him love her. It would seem to him a wicked thing and he would not love her truly. And she would no longer matter to him or anyone else.

The priest would revile her. She would be of no use to him and he would know that she had acted wrongly and selfishly. All his kindness to her and his hard work in teaching her would have meant less to her than being Nogaro's wife.

Halana wept. She longed to have the spirit of the great fruit tree come and tell her what to do and how to do it, how to make Nogaro choose her and still be a witch, someone able to be of service to her town, someone deserving of admiration and respect. But the spirit did not come.

And when darkness descended, Halana lay down upon the earth and wept still more, for she felt the icy wind and knew there was no help for her. And she implored the spirit to come and comfort her, but there was no response.

After two days she went back to the village. She went slowly, for the pain in her heart was great and seemed to make her limbs heavy and weary. When she returned to her house, Nogaro's father was waiting for her. He came to meet her and looked at her anxiously.

"Have I asked so much of you?" he asked. "You seem ill. Is this such a difficult task?"

"I am not ill," answered Halana. "The task you set me is not too difficult. I will do as you have requested. It will take a few days."

Nogaro's father was pleased. But Halana did not have to use her powers on Nogaro. The next day he went to Tadar and asked permission to marry his daughter Manika.

Halana went to the marriage and she wished them well, for they were strong and handsome and good and suited each other nicely. She hoped that all they did would thrive and prosper.

And Halana herself went about the affairs of her craft quietly and earnestly. She cured those who were ill and comforted children who had bad dreams and caused gardens to grow well.

And after some time she knew that the spirit of the great fruit tree, by its very silence, had given her wise advice.

She cured a man who suffered from terrible headaches and helped a woman locate her favorite needle, which had been lost, and called forth warm weather in a lazy spring.

And after some time she knew that Dita was truly gone, that she was truly Halana, and she was happy again.

OLIVER HYDE'S DISHCLOTH CONCERT

Richard Kennedy

Now maybe it's sad and maybe it's spooky, but there was a man who lived just out of town on a scrubby farm and no one had seen his face for years. If he was outside working, he kept his hat pulled down and his collar turned up, and if anyone approached him he ran up the hill to his house and shut himself inside. He left notes pinned to his door for a brave errand boy who brought him supplies from town. The people asked the boy what he heard up there in that tomblike house when he collected the notes and delivered the supplies. "Darkness and quietness," said the boy. "I hear darkness and quietness." The people nodded and looked at the boy. "Aren't you afraid?" The boy bit his lip. "A fellow has to make a living," he said.

Sometimes the children would come out of town and sing a little song up at the house and then run away. They sang:

> "The beautiful bride of Oliver Hyde,
> Fell down dead on the mountainside."

Yes, it was true. The man was full of grief and bitterness. He was Oliver Hyde, and his young bride's wagon had been washed into a canyon by a mudslide and it killed her, horse and all. But that was years ago. The children sang some more:

> "Oliver Hyde is a strange old man,
> He sticks his head in a coffee can,
> And hides his face when there's folks about,
> He's outside in, and he's inside out."

It was too bad. Oliver used to have many friends, and he played the fastest and sweetest fiddle in the county. And for the few short weeks he was married his playing was sweeter than ever. But on the day his wife was buried he busted his fiddle across a porch post, and now he sat cold, dark, and quiet on his little hill. No one had visited him for years. There was a reason. You shall see.

One day a man came from the town and walked up the hill toward Oliver's house. He was carrying a fiddle case. Two or three times he stopped and looked up at the house and shook his head, as if trying to free himself from a ghost, and continued on. He arrived at the porch steps. All the window shades were pulled down and it was dead quiet inside. The three porch steps creaked like cats moaning in their dreams, and the man knocked on the door. For a little bit it was quiet, then there was the sound of a chair being scooted across the floor. A voice said, "Come in."

The man opened the door a crack and peeked inside.

"Oliver?" he said. "It's me, Jim." No answer. Jim opened the door farther and put a foot inside. It was dark, and smelled stale. Jim opened the door all the way.

Off in a corner where the light didn't touch sat a figure in a chair, perfectly upright, with his hands on his knees like a stone god, as still and silent as a thousand years ago. The head was draped completely with a dishcloth. Not a breath ruffled the ghost head.

Jim swallowed and spoke. "Haven't seen you around lately, Oliver." No answer.

People used to visit Oliver for a while after his beautiful bride fell down dead on the mountainside, but this is how it was—Oliver sitting in the dark with a dishcloth over his head, and he never spoke to them. It was too strange. His friends stopped visiting.

All Jim wanted was a single word from Oliver—yes or no. He had a favor to ask. He was Oliver's oldest friend. He moved inside.

"Sue's getting married, Oliver," he said. No answer. "You remember my little girl, Sue? She's all growed up now, Oliver, and mighty pretty, too." For all the notice he got, Jim might just as well have been talking to a stove. He cleared his voice and went on. "The reason I came, Oliver, was to ask you to come and play the fiddle for us at the dance. We was the best friends, and I don't see how I can marry off Sue without you being there to fiddle for us. You can just say yes or no, Oliver."

Now Oliver wasn't dead himself yet, so he still had feelings, and Jim had been his best friend. They had played and fought together, fished and hunted, and grown up together. So Oliver hated to say "No" just flat out like that, so he said instead, "No fiddle." Jim was prepared for that, and he laid the fiddle case down on the floor and flipped it open.

"Here, I brought a fiddle, Oliver. Porky Fellows was happy to make a lend of it."

Oliver felt trapped now. He was silent for a long time, then finally he said, "Tell you what. I can't wear this dishcloth on my head and fiddle, but if everyone else wears a dishcloth I'll come."

Jim was quiet for a long time, but at last he said, "All right, Oliver, I'll ask if they'll do it. The dance is tomorrow night at Edward's barn. I'll leave the fiddle here, and if I don't come back to pick it up, then you got to come to the dance and fiddle for us. I got your promise."

Oliver smiled under his dishcloth. They'd be fools to agree to that. You can't have any fun with a dishcloth over your head.

"So long, Oliver," Jim said. Oliver didn't answer. Jim went back on down the hill.

Oliver took the dishcloth off. The fiddle was laying in the light of the open door. He sucked a whisker and looked at it. Oliver knew the fiddle, and it was a good fiddle. He wondered if it was in tune and wanted to pick it up, but he let it lay there. His foot was tapping, and he slapped his knee to make it stop. He laughed to himself and muttered, "Them donkeys—what do they know?" Then he got up and moved around the little house on his dreary business.

The sun went down and the shadow of the fiddle case stretched across the floor. Oliver's eyes kept landing on the fiddle, and he stepped over the shadow when he crossed that way. It looked to him like the bow had new horsehair on it. But it didn't make any difference to him. He figured he'd never be playing on that fiddle, and he never touched it.

Next morning Oliver watched down the hill for Jim to come and tell him the deal was off and to get the fiddle. Noon came. Oliver ate some beans. Afternoon came on. Jim didn't show. Oliver began to get mad. He was mad that he had ever made the promise. It started to get dark. "Those cluckheads!" Oliver said, pulling the window shut. "They can't dance with dishcloths on their heads, or drink punch, either. They'll have a rotten time."

But a promise is a promise.

Finally he decided it was time to put his hat and coat on. "They tricked me," Oliver grumbled, "but I got a trick for them, too. They'll be sorry I came to their party." It wasn't a great trick Oliver had in mind, but just a miserable little one to make sure nobody could have any fun while he was there. He figured they'd ask him to leave shortly. He wouldn't even bother to take off his hat and coat.

He headed down the hill with the fiddle and into the little town. He entered Edward's barn with his hat pulled down and his collar turned up. It was dark except for two bare, hanging light bulbs, one over the center of the barn and one at the end where a sort of stage was built up. Oliver had played at shindigs there many times. He kept his head down, and only from the corners of his eyes could he see all the people sitting around the walls. "Lord, it's awfully dark," Oliver thought to himself, "and quiet. I figure they know that's the way I like it." He got under the light bulb that hung over the stage and took out the fiddle.

He tuned down to a fretful and lonesome sound, and then he played.

Of course he knew they were all looking for happy dancing tunes, so first off he played a slow and sad tune about a man who was walking down a long road that had no ending and was gray all about, and the man was looking forward to being dead because it might be more cheerful. Nobody danced, naturally, and didn't clap either when Oliver finished it. "That's just right," Oliver thought. "I'll give them a wretched time." And he started on another.

The second tune he played was even slower and sadder, about a man who thought his heart was a pincushion and it seemed to him that everyone was sticking pins and needles into it, and it was hurtful even to listen to it. Nobody danced, and nobody even moved to the punch bowl to get their spirits up. "Now they're sorry I came," Oliver thought. Still, he had played that last tune especially sweet, and he expected someone might have clapped a little just for that, even if it was sad.

Oliver looked out a little under his hat as he retuned a bit. He tried to see Jim. He ought to come up and say hello at least, not just let him stand there completely alone. And he wondered where the other musicians were. Four people were sitting down off to the right of the stage. That would be them. Oliver considered it would be nice to have a little slide guitar on these slow ones, sort of mournful played, and a mouth harp and mandolin would fit in nice. "Naw! This is just the way I want it. One more gloomy song and they'll ask me to leave."

So then he played another, this one about a man who had a wife that just recently moved to heaven, and how roses grew all over her tombstone even in the winter. Oliver was halfway through that before he remembered that he'd played that tune at his own wedding party. He pulled up short a bit then, but kept on playing it out, and a tear rolled down his cheek. Well, nobody could see. He wiped his eyes when he was finished.

Nobody clapped and nobody moved, just sat against the dark walls perfectly still. Among the dark figures was a lighter shape. Probably the bride in her white gown. Oliver remembered how lovely and happy his bride had been, and he felt a little mean when he thought about that, giving out such sad tunes.

He spoke out loud, the first words that were spoken since he came in. "Well, I guess you're all ready for me to leave now, and I will. But first I want to play just one happy tune for the bride, and so you can dance, and then I'll go." Then he did play a happy one, a fast one, carrying on with fiddling lively enough to scramble eggs. But nobody got up to dance, and when he was finished nobody moved or made a sound.

"Look here," Oliver said. "I reckon you can't dance with those dishcloths over your heads, I forgot about that. So take 'em off. I'll give you another dancing tune, then I'll go." And then he went into another, as sweet and light and fast as anyone ever could, something to get even a rock up and dancing, but nobody moved. And when he was finished they all sat silent with the dishcloths still on their heads.

"Come on," Oliver said. "Take those things off your heads. You other fellows get up here with your music and help me out. Let's have some dancing, drink some punch, let's get alive now." He stomped his foot three times and threw into a tune that would churn butter all by itself. But the other four musicians sat perfectly still, and so did everybody else, and Oliver was standing there under the light bulb in silence when he finished the tune.

He stood there with his head down, understanding things, and how it felt to be on the other side of the darkness and silence when all you wanted was some sign of life to help out. Then he leaned over and put the fiddle in the case and closed it. He said one last thing, then walked out from under the light toward the door. "Okay," he said. "That's a hard lesson, but I got it."

When he opened the door he bumped into someone sitting next to it against the wall, and the fellow fell off his chair. Oliver put a hand down to help him up. But the fellow just lay there. Oliver touched him. "What's this?" He felt around, then shoved back his hat for a look. It was a sack of grain he'd knocked over. And the next person sitting there was a sack of grain, too. And the next was a bale of hay.

Oliver walked completely around the barn. All the people were sacks of grain and bales of hay sitting against the dark walls, and the bride was a white sack of flour. The four musicians sitting off to the right of the stage were four old saddles setting on a rail.

When Oliver came around to the door again he heard music. He stepped outside and looked down the street. A barn down near the end was all lit up, and lots of people were moving about. He went back up on the stage, got the fiddle, and headed down the street.

Jim was standing by the door. "Waiting for you, Oliver," he said. "We're just getting under way—come on in." When he led Oliver inside everyone became quiet, first one little group of people then another, until at last everyone was silent and looking at Oliver. The bride and groom were holding hands. Jim made a motion and everyone headed for a chair against the walls. They all took out dishcloths to put over their heads.

"Edward's got himself a new barn, huh?" Oliver said.

"Yeah," said Jim. "I guess you didn't know that. Uses the old one to store stuff. I shoulda told you."

"It's all right," Oliver said. He looked up on the stage. Four musicians were sitting there with dishcloths over their heads. Then Jim took out a large dishcloth. Oliver touched him on the arm.

"Never mind that. And everyone else, too. Just be regular and dance. I'll fiddle for you."

Jim slapped him on the back and shouted out the good news. Oliver went up on the stage. Someone got him a mug of punch. The musicians tuned up. Oliver took off his hat and dropped it, and tossed his coat on a chair. They lit into a fast, happy tune. They danced and played and sang half the night.

Ah, they had a wonderful time. Oliver included.

CHARACTERS IN "THE JUNGLE BOOKS"

(pronunciations based on the Hindi)

AKELA [A-*kay*-la] The leader of the Seeonee wolf pack when Mowgli comes to the jungle as a baby; also called the Lone Wolf.

BAGHEERA [Bag-eera, pronounced like an "era" in history] The black panther who, for the price of a newly slain bull, bought the infant Mowgli's acceptance into the Seeonee wolf pack.

BALOO [*Bar*-loo] The wise, old brown bear who teaches wolf cubs the Law of the Jungle. He, along with Bagheera, spoke in favor of admitting Mowgli into the Seeonee wolf pack.

BANDAR-LOG [Bunder-logue] The Monkey-people.

BULDEO [*Bul*-doo] The village hunter who led the movement to cast Mowgli out.

CHIL [Cheel] The kite, a bird of prey and a scavenger.

DHOLE [Dole] A fierce, wild red dog of India.

FERAO [Feer-*ow*] The scarlet woodpecker.

HATHI [Huttee] The elephant, also called the Silent One.

KAA [Kar, with a sort of gasp in it] The rock python who befriends Mowgli; head of the Middle Jungle.

MESSUA [*Mes*-war] Mowgli's human mother.

MOWGLI ["Mow" rhymes with "cow"] The boy who grows up as a wolf in the jungles of India.

MYSA [*Mi*-sar] The wild buffalo.

NATHOO [Nut-too] Messua's name for Mowgli.

RAKSHA [*Ruck*-sher] "The Demon"—Mowgli's wolf mother. Her children, including Grey Brother, are known as the Four.

SEEONEE [See-*own*-y] The name of Mowgli's wolf pack.

SHERE KHAN [Sheer Karn] The tiger who hunted Mowgli and whom Mowgli eventually slays; also called Lungri, the Lame One.

TABAQUI [Ta-*bar*-kee] The jackal, a follower of Shere Khan; also called Dish-licker.

MOWGLI'S BROTHERS

Rudyard Kipling

It was seven o'clock of a very warm evening in the Seeonee Hills when Father Wolf woke up from his day's rest, scratched himself, yawned, and spread out his paws one after the other to get rid of the sleepy feeling in their tips. Mother Wolf lay with her big grey nose dropped across her four tumbling, squealing cubs, and the moon shone into the mouth of the cave where they all lived. "*Augrh!*" said Father Wolf, "it is time to hunt again." And he was going to spring down hill when a little shadow with a bushy tail crossed the threshold and whined: "Good luck go with you, O Chief of the Wolves; and good luck and strong white teeth go with the noble children, that they may never forget the hungry in this world."

It was the jackal—Tabaqui the Dish-licker—and the wolves of India despise Tabaqui because he runs about making mischief, and telling tales, and eating rags and pieces of leather from the village rubbish heaps. But they are afraid of him too, because Tabaqui, more than anyone else in the jungle, is apt to go mad, and then he forgets that he was ever afraid of anyone, and runs through the forest biting everything in his way. Even the tiger runs and hides when little Tabaqui goes mad, for madness is the most disgraceful thing that can overtake a wild creature. We call it hydrophobia, but they call it *dewanee*—the madness—and run.

"Enter, then, and look," said Father Wolf, stiffly, "but there is no food here."

"For a wolf, no," said Tabaqui, "but for so mean a person as myself a dry bone is a good feast. Who are we, the *Gidur-log* [the Jackal-People], to pick and choose?" He scuttled to the back of the cave, where he found the bone of a buck with some meat on it, and sat cracking the end merrily.

"All thanks for this good meal," he said, licking his lips. "How beautiful are the noble children! How large are their eyes! And so young too! Indeed, indeed, I might have remembered that the children of kings are men from the beginning."

Now, Tabaqui knew as well as anyone else that there is nothing so unlucky as to compliment children to their faces; and it pleased him to see Mother and Father Wolf look uncomfortable.

Tabaqui sat still, rejoicing in the mischief that he had made, and then he said spitefully:

"Shere Khan, the Big One, has shifted his hunting grounds. He will hunt among these hills for the next moon, so he has told me."

Shere Khan was the tiger who lived near the Wainganga River, twenty miles away.

"He has no right!" Father Wolf began angrily. "By the Law of the Jungle he has no right to change his quarters without due warning. He will frighten every head of game within ten miles, and I—I have to kill for two, these days."

"His mother did not call him Lungri [the Lame One] for nothing," said Mother Wolf, quietly. "He has been lame in one foot from his birth. That is why he has only killed cattle. Now the villagers of the Wainganga are angry with him, and he has come here to make *our* villagers angry. They will scour the jungle for him when he is far away, and we and our children must run when the grass is set alight. Indeed, we are very grateful to Shere Khan!"

"Shall I tell him of your gratitude?" said Tabaqui.

"Out!" snapped Father Wolf. "Out and hunt with thy master. Thou hast done harm enough for one night."

"I go," said Tabaqui, quietly. "Ye can hear Shere Khan below in the thickets. I might have saved myself the message."

Father Wolf listened, and below in the valley that ran down to a little river, he heard the dry, angry, snarly, singsong whine of a tiger who has caught nothing and does not care if all the jungle knows it.

"The fool!" said Father Wolf. "To begin a night's work with that noise! Does he think that our buck are like his fat Wainganga bullocks?"

"*Hsh.* It is neither bullock nor buck he hunts tonight," said Mother Wolf. "It is Man." The whine had changed to a sort of humming purr that seemed to come from every quarter of the compass. It was the noise that bewilders woodcutters and gypsies sleeping in the open, and makes them run sometimes into the very mouth of the tiger.

"Man!" said Father Wolf, showing all his white teeth. "*Faugh!* Are there not enough beetles and frogs in the tanks that he must eat Man, and on our ground too!"

The Law of the Jungle, which never orders anything without a reason, forbids every beast to eat Man except when he is killing to show his children how to kill, and then he must hunt outside the hunting grounds of his pack or tribe. The real reason for this is that man-killing means, sooner or later, the arrival of white men on elephants, with guns, and hundreds of brown men with gongs and rockets and torches. Then everybody in the jungle suffers. The reason the beasts give among themselves is that Man is the weakest and most defenseless of all living things, and it is unsportsmanlike to touch him. They say too—and it is true—that maneaters become mangy, and lose their teeth.

The purr grew louder, and ended in the full-throated "*Aaarh!*" of the tiger's charge.

Then there was a howl—an untigerish howl—from Shere Khan. "He has missed," said Mother Wolf. "What is it?"

Father Wolf ran out a few paces and heard Shere Khan muttering and mumbling savagely, as he tumbled about in the scrub.

"The fool has had no more sense than to jump at a woodcutters' campfire, and has burned his feet," said Father Wolf, with a grunt. "Tabaqui is with him."

"Something is coming up hill," said Mother Wolf, twitching one ear. "Get ready."

The bushes rustled a little in the thicket, and Father Wolf dropped with his haunches under him, ready for his leap. Then, if you had been watching, you would have seen the most wonderful thing in the world—the wolf checked in mid-spring. He made his bound before he saw what it was he was jumping at, and then he tried to stop himself. The result was that he shot up straight into the air for four or five feet, landing almost where he left ground.

"Man!" he snapped. "A man's cub. Look!"

Directly in front of him, holding on by a low branch, stood a naked brown baby who could just walk—as soft and as dimpled a little atom as ever came to a wolf's cave at night. He looked up into Father Wolf's face, and laughed.

"Is that a man's cub?" said Mother Wolf. "I have never seen one. Bring it here."

A wolf accustomed to moving his own cubs can, if necessary, mouth an egg without breaking it, and though Father Wolf's jaws closed right on the child's back, not a tooth even scratched the skin, as he laid it down among the cubs.

"How little! How naked, and—how bold!" said Mother Wolf, softly. The baby was pushing his way between the cubs to get close to the warm hide. "*Ahai!* He is taking his meal with the others. And so this is a man's cub. Now, was there ever a wolf that could boast of a man's cub among her children?"

"I have heard now and again of such a thing, but never in our pack or in my time," said Father Wolf. "He is altogether without hair, and I could kill him with a touch of my foot. But see, he looks up and is not afraid."

The moonlight was blocked out of the mouth of the cave, for Shere Khan's great square head and shoulders were thrust into the entrance. Tabaqui, behind him, was squeaking: "My lord, my lord, it went in here!"

"Shere Khan does us great honour," said Father Wolf, but his eyes were very angry. "What does Shere Khan need?"

"My quarry. A man's cub went this way," said Shere Khan. "Its parents have run off. Give it to me."

Shere Khan had jumped at a woodcutter's campfire, as Father Wolf had said, and was furious from the pain of his burned feet. But Father Wolf knew that the mouth of the cave was too narrow for a tiger to come in by. Even where he was, Shere Khan's shoulders and forepaws were cramped for want of room, as a man's would be if he tried to fight in a barrel.

"The wolves are a free people," said Father Wolf. "They take orders from the head of the pack, and not from any striped cattle killer. The man's cub is ours—to kill if we choose."

"Ye choose and ye do not choose! What talk is this of choosing? By the bull that I killed, am I to stand nosing into your dog's den for my fair dues? It is I, Shere Khan, who speak!"

The tiger's roar filled the cave with thunder. Mother Wolf shook herself clear of the cubs and sprang forward, her eyes, like two green moons in the darkness, facing the blazing eyes of Shere Khan.

"And it is I, Raksha [the Demon], who answer. The man's cub is mine, Lungri—mine to me! He shall not be killed. He shall live to run with the pack and to hunt with the pack; and in the end, look you, hunter of little naked cubs—frog-eater—fish-killer—he shall hunt *thee*! Now get hence, or by the sambur that I killed (*I* eat no starved cattle), back thou goest to thy mother, burned beast of the jungle, lamer than ever thou camest into the world! Go!"

Father Wolf looked on amazed. He had almost forgotten the days when he won Mother Wolf in fair fight from five other wolves, when she ran in the pack and was not called the Demon for compliment's sake. Shere Khan might have faced Father Wolf, but he could not stand up against Mother Wolf, for he knew that where he was she had all the advantage of the ground, and would fight to the death. So he backed out of the cave mouth growling, and when he was clear he shouted:

"Each dog barks in his own yard! We will see what the pack will say to this fostering of man-cubs. The cub is mine, and to my teeth he will come in the end, O bushtailed thieves!"

Mother Wolf threw herself down panting among the cubs, and Father Wolf said to her gravely:

"Shere Khan speaks this much truth. The cub must be shown to the pack. Wilt thou still keep him, Mother?"

"Keep him!" she gasped. "He came naked, by night, alone and very hungry; yet he was not afraid! Look, he has pushed one of my babes to one side already. And that lame butcher would have killed him and would have run off to the Wainganga while the villagers here hunted through all our lairs in revenge! Keep him? Assuredly I will keep him. Lie still, little frog. O thou Mowgli—for Mowgli the Frog I will call thee—the time will come when thou wilt hunt Shere Khan as he has hunted thee."

"But what will our pack say?" said Father Wolf.

The Law of the Jungle lays down very clearly that any wolf may, when he marries, withdraw from the pack he belongs to; but as soon as his cubs are old enough to stand on their feet he must bring them to the pack council, which is generally held once a month at full moon, in order that the other wolves may identify them. After that inspection the cubs are free to run where they please, and until they have killed their first buck no excuse is accepted if a grown wolf of the pack kills one of them. The punishment is death where the murderer can be found; and if you think for a minute, you will see that this must be so.

Father Wolf waited till his cubs could run a little, and then on the night of the pack meeting took them and Mowgli and Mother Wolf to the Council Rock—a hilltop covered with stones and boulders where a hundred wolves could hide. Akela, the great grey Lone Wolf, who led all the pack by strength and cunning, lay out at full length on his rock, and below him sat forty or more wolves of every size and colour, from badger-coloured veterans who could handle a buck alone, to young black three-year-olds who thought they could. The Lone Wolf had led them for a year now. He had fallen twice into a wolf-trap in his youth, and once he had been beaten and left for dead; so he knew the manners and customs of men. There was very little talking at the rock. The cubs tumbled over each other in the centre of the circle where their mothers and fathers sat, and now and again a senior wolf would go quietly up to a cub, look at him carefully, and return to his place on noiseless feet. Sometimes a mother would push her cub far out into the moonlight, to be sure that he had not been overlooked. Akela from his rock would cry: "Ye know the Law—ye know the Law. Look well, O wolves!" And the anxious mothers would take up the call: "Look—look well, O wolves!"

At last—and Mother Wolf's neck-bristles lifted as the time came—Father Wolf pushed "Mowgli the Frog," as they called him, into the centre, where he sat laughing and playing with some pebbles that glistened in the moonlight.

Akela never raised his head from his paws, but went on with the monotonous cry: "Look well!" A muffled roar came up from behind the rocks—the voice of Shere Khan crying: "The cub is mine. Give him to me. What have the Free People to do with a man's cub?" Akela never even twitched his ears. All he said was: "Look well, O wolves! What have the Free People to do with the orders of any save the Free People? Look well!"

There was a chorus of deep growls, and a young wolf in his fourth year flung back Shere Khan's question to Akela: "What have the Free People to do with a man's cub?" Now the Law of the Jungle lays down that if there is any dispute as to the right of a cub to be accepted by the pack, he must be spoken for by at least two members of the pack who are not his father and mother.

"Who speaks for this cub?" said Akela. "Among the Free People who speaks?" There was no answer, and Mother Wolf got ready for what she knew would be her last fight, if things came to fighting.

Then the only other creature who is allowed at the pack council—Baloo, the sleepy brown bear who teaches the wolf cubs the Law of the Jungle: old Baloo, who can come and go where he pleases because he eats only nuts and roots and honey—rose up on his hindquarters and grunted.

"The man's cub—the man's cub?" he said. "*I* speak for the man's cub. There is no harm in a man's cub. I have no gift of words, but I speak the truth. Let him run with the pack, and be entered with the others. I myself will teach him."

"We need yet another," said Akela. "Baloo has spoken, and he is our teacher for the young cubs. Who speaks besides Baloo?"

A black shadow dropped down into the circle. It was Bagheera the Black Panther, inky black all over, but with the panther markings showing up in certain lights like the pattern of watered silk. Everybody knew Bagheera, and nobody cared to cross his path, for he was as cunning as Tabaqui, as bold as the wild buffalo, and as reckless as the wounded elephant. But he had a voice as soft as wild honey dripping from a tree, and a skin softer than down.

"O Akela, and ye the Free People," he purred, "I have no right in your assembly, but the Law of the Jungle says that if there is a doubt which is not a killing matter in regard to a new cub, the life of that cub may be bought at a price. And the Law does not say who may or may not pay that price. Am I right?"

"Good! Good!" said the young wolves, who are always hungry. "Listen to Bagheera. The cub can be bought for a price. It is the Law."

"Knowing that I have no right to speak here, I ask your leave."

"Speak then," cried twenty voices.

"To kill a naked cub is shame. Besides, he may make better sport for you when he is grown. Baloo has spoken in his behalf. Now to Baloo's word I will add one bull, and a fat one, newly killed, not half a mile from here, if ye will accept the man's cub according to the Law. Is it difficult?"

There was a clamour of scores of voices, saying: "What matter? He will die in the winter rains. He will scorch in the sun. What harm can a naked frog do us? Let him run with the pack. Where is the bull, Bagheera? Let him be accepted." And then came Akela's deep bay, crying: "Look well—look well, O wolves!"

Mowgli was still deeply interested in the pebbles, and he did not notice when the wolves came and looked at him one by one. At last they all went down the hill for the dead bull, and only Akela, Bagheera, Baloo, and Mowgli's own wolves were left. Shere Khan roared still in the night, for he was very angry that Mowgli had not been handed over to him.

"Aye, roar well," said Bagheera, under his whiskers, "for the time comes when this naked thing will make thee roar to another tune, or I know nothing of Man."

"It was well done," said Akela. "Men and their cubs are very wise. He may be a help in time."

"Truly, a help in time of need, for none can hope to lead the pack forever," said Bagheera.

Akela said nothing. He was thinking of the time that comes to every leader of every pack when his strength goes from him and he gets feebler and feebler, till at last he is killed by the wolves and a new leader comes up—to be killed in his turn.

"Take him away," he said to Father Wolf, "and train him as befits one of the Free People."

And that is how Mowgli was entered into the Seeonee Wolf Pack for the price of a bull and on Baloo's good word.

Now you must be content to skip ten or eleven whole years, and only guess at all the wonderful life that Mowgli led among the wolves, because if it were written out it would fill ever so many books. He grew up with the cubs, though they, of course, were grown wolves almost before he was a child, and Father Wolf taught him his business, and the meaning of things in the jungle, till every rustle in the grass, every breath of the warm night air, every note of the owls above his head, every scratch of a bat's claws as it roosted for a while in a tree, and every splash of every little fish jumping in a pool, meant just as much to him as the work of his office means to a businessman. When he was not learning he sat out in the sun and slept, and ate and went to sleep again; when he felt dirty or hot he swam in the forest pools; and when he wanted honey (Baloo told him that honey and nuts were just as pleasant to eat as raw meat) he climbed up for it, and that Bagheera showed him how to do. Bagheera would lie out on a branch and call: "Come along, Little Brother," and at first Mowgli would cling like the sloth, but afterwards he would fling himself through the branches almost as boldly as the grey ape. He took his place at the Council Rock, too, when the pack met, and there he discovered that if he stared hard at any wolf, the wolf would be forced to drop his eyes, and so he used to stare for fun. At other times he would pick the long thorns out of the pads of his friends, for wolves suffer terribly from thorns and burs in their coats. He would go down the hillside into the cultivated lands by night, and look very curiously at the villagers in their huts, but he had a mistrust of men because Bagheera showed him a square box with a drop-gate so cunningly hidden in the jungle that he nearly walked into it, and told him that it was a trap. He loved better than anything else to go with Bagheera into the dark warm heart of the forest, to sleep all through the drowsy day, and at night see how Bagheera did his killing. Bagheera killed right and left as he felt hungry, and so did Mowgli—with one exception. As soon as he was old enough to understand things, Bagheera told him that he must never touch cattle because he had been bought into the pack at the price of a bull's life. "All the jungle is thine," said Bagheera, "and thou canst kill everything that thou art strong enough to kill; but for the sake of the bull that bought thee thou must never kill or eat any cattle young or old. That is the Law of the Jungle." Mowgli obeyed faithfully.

And he grew and grew strong as a boy must grow who does not know that he is learning any lessons, and who has nothing in the world to think of except things to eat.

Mother Wolf told him once or twice that Shere Khan was not a creature to be trusted, and that someday he must kill Shere Khan. But though a young wolf would have remembered that advice every hour, Mowgli forgot it because he was only a boy—though he would have called himself a wolf if he had been able to speak in any human tongue.

Shere Khan was always crossing his path in the jungle, for as Akela grew older and feebler the lame tiger had come to be great friends with the younger wolves of the pack, who followed him for scraps, a thing Akela would never have allowed if he had dared to push his authority to the proper bounds. Then Shere Khan would flatter them and wonder that such fine young hunters were content to be led by a dying wolf and a man's cub. "They tell me," Shere Khan would say, "that at council ye dare not look him between the eyes." And the young wolves would growl and bristle.

Bagheera, who had eyes and ears everywhere, knew something of this, and once or twice he told Mowgli in so many words that Shere Khan would kill him someday. And Mowgli would laugh and answer: "I have the pack and I have thee; and Baloo, though he is so lazy, might strike a blow or two for my sake. Why should I be afraid?"

It was one very warm day that a new notion came to Bagheera—born of something that he had heard. Perhaps Sahi the Porcupine had told him; but he said to Mowgli when they were deep in the jungle, as the boy lay with his head on Bagheera's beautiful black skin: "Little Brother, how often have I told thee that Shere Khan is thy enemy?"

"As many times as there are nuts on that palm," said Mowgli, who, naturally, could not count. "What of it? I am sleepy, Bagheera, and Shere Khan is all long tail and loud talk—like Mor the Peacock."

"But this is no time for sleeping. Baloo knows it; I know it; the pack knows it; and even the foolish, foolish deer know. Tabaqui has told thee, too."

"Ho! Ho!" said Mowgli. "Tabaqui came to me not long ago with some rude talk that I was a naked man's cub and not fit to dig pig-nuts; but I caught Tabaqui by the tail and swung him twice against a palm tree to teach him better manners."

"That was foolishness, for though Tabaqui is a mischief maker, he would have told thee of something that concerned thee closely. Open those eyes, Little Brother. Shere Khan dare not kill thee in the jungle; but remember, Akela is very old, and soon the day comes when he cannot kill his buck, and then he will be leader no more. Many of the wolves that looked thee over when thou wast brought to the council first are old too, and the young wolves believe, as Shere Khan has taught them, that a man-cub has no place with the pack. In a little time thou wilt be a man."

"And what is a man that he should not run with his brothers?" said Mowgli. "I was born in the jungle. I have obeyed the Law of the Jungle, and there is no wolf of ours from whose paws I have not pulled a thorn. Surely they are my brothers!"

Bagheera stretched himself at full length and half shut his eyes. "Little Brother," said he, "feel under my jaw."

Mowgli put up his strong brown hand, and just under Bagheera's silky chin, where the giant rolling muscles were all hid by the glossy hair, he came upon a little bald spot.

"There is no one in the jungle that knows that I, Bagheera, carry that mark—the mark of the collar. And yet, Little Brother, I was born among men, and it was among men that my mother died—in the cages of the king's palace at Oodeypore. It was because of this that I paid the price for thee at the council when thou wast a little naked cub. Yes, I too was born among men. I had never seen the jungle. They fed me behind bars from an iron pan till one night I felt that I was Bagheera—the Panther—and no man's plaything, and I broke the silly lock with one blow of my paw and came away. And because I had learned the ways of men, I became more terrible in the jungle than Shere Khan. Is it not so?"

"Yes," said Mowgli, "all the jungle fears Bagheera—all except Mowgli."

"Oh, *thou* art a man's cub," said the black panther, very tenderly, "and even as I returned to my jungle, so thou must go back to men at last—to the men who are thy brothers—if thou art not killed in the council."

"But why—but why should any wish to kill me?" said Mowgli.

"Look at me," said Bagheera, and Mowgli looked at him steadily between the eyes. The big panther turned his head away in half a minute.

"*That* is why," he said, shifting his paw on the leaves. "Not even I can look thee between the eyes, and I was born among men, and I love thee, Little Brother. The others they hate thee because their eyes cannot meet thine; because thou art wise; because thou hast pulled out thorns from their feet—because thou art a man."

"I did not know these things," said Mowgli, sullenly, and he frowned under his heavy black eyebrows.

"What is the Law of the Jungle? Strike first and then give tongue. By thy very carelessness they know that thou art a man. But be wise. It is in my heart that when Akela misses his next kill—and at each hunt it costs him more to pin the buck—the pack will turn against him and against thee. They will hold a jungle council at the rock, and then—and then—I have it!" said Bagheera, leaping up. "Go thou down quickly to the men's huts in the valley, and take some of the Red Flower which they grow there, so that when the time comes thou mayest have even a stronger friend than I or Baloo or those of the pack that love thee. Get the Red Flower."

By Red Flower Bagheera meant fire, only no creature in the jungle will call fire by its proper name. Every beast lives in deadly fear of it, and invents a hundred ways of describing it.

"The Red Flower?" said Mowgli. "That grows outside their huts in the twilight. I will get some."

"There speaks the man's cub," said Bagheera, proudly. "Remember that it grows in little pots. Get one swiftly, and keep it by thee for time of need."

"Good!" said Mowgli. "I go. But art thou sure, O my Bagheera"—he slipped his arm round the splendid neck, and looked deep into the big eyes—"art thou sure that all this is Shere Khan's doing?"

"By the broken lock that freed me, I am sure, Little Brother."

"Then, by the bull that bought me, I will pay Shere Khan full tale for this, and it may be a little over," said Mowgli, and he bounded away.

"That is a man. That is all a man," said Bagheera to himself, lying down again. "Oh, Shere Khan, never was a blacker hunting than that frog-hunt of thine ten years ago!"

Mowgli was far and far through the forest, running hard, and his heart was hot in him. He came to the cave as the evening mist rose, and drew breath, and looked down the valley. The cubs were out, but Mother Wolf, at the back of the cave, knew by his breathing that something was troubling her frog.

"What is it, Son?" she said.

"Some bat's chatter of Shere Khan," he called back. "I hunt among the ploughed fields tonight." And he plunged downward through the bushes, to the stream at the bottom of the valley. There he checked, for he heard the yell of the pack hunting, heard the bellow of a hunted sambur, and the snort as the buck turned at bay.

Then there were wicked, bitter howls from the young wolves: "Akela! Akela! Let the Lone Wolf show his strength. Room for the leader of the pack! Spring, Akela!"

The Lone Wolf must have sprung and missed his hold, for Mowgli heard the snap of his teeth and then a yelp as the sambur knocked him over with his forefoot.

He did not wait for anything more, but dashed on; and the yells grew fainter behind him as he ran into the crop lands where the villagers lived.

"Bagheera spoke truth," he panted, as he nestled down in some cattle fodder by the window of a hut. "Tomorrow is one day both for Akela and for me."

Then he pressed his face close to the window and watched the fire on the hearth. He saw the husbandman's wife get up and feed it in the night with black lumps; and when the morning came and the mists were all white and cold, he saw the man's child pick up a wicker pot plastered inside with earth, fill it with lumps of red-hot charcoal, put it under his blanket, and go out to tend the cows in the byre.

"Is that all?" said Mowgli. "If a cub can do it, there is nothing to fear." So he strode round the corner and met the boy, took the pot from his hand, and disappeared into the mist while the boy howled with fear.

"They are very like me," said Mowgli, blowing into the pot, as he had seen the woman do. "This thing will die if I do not give it things to eat." And he dropped twigs and dried bark on the red stuff. Halfway up the hill he met Bagheera with the morning dew shining like moonstones on his coat.

"Akela has missed," said the panther. "They would have killed him last night, but they needed thee also. They were looking for thee on the hill."

"I was among the ploughed lands. I am ready. See!" Mowgli held up the fire-pot.

"Good! Now, I have seen men thrust a dry branch into that stuff, and presently the Red Flower blossomed at the end of it. Art thou not afraid?"

"No. Why should I fear? I remember now—if it is not a dream—how, before I was a wolf, I lay beside the Red Flower, and it was warm and pleasant."

All that day Mowgli sat in the cave tending his fire-pot and dipping dry branches into it to see how they looked. He found a branch that satisfied him, and in the evening when Tabaqui came to the cave and told him rudely enough that he was wanted at the Council Rock, he laughed till Tabaqui ran away. Then Mowgli went to the council, still laughing.

Akela the Lone Wolf lay by the side of his rock as a sign that the leadership of the pack was open, and Shere Khan with his following of scrap-fed wolves walked to and fro openly being flattered. Bagheera lay close to Mowgli, and the fire-pot was between Mowgli's knees. When they were all gathered together, Shere Khan began to speak—a thing he would never have dared to do when Akela was in his prime.

"He has no right," whispered Bagheera. "Say so. He is a dog's son. He will be frightened."

Mowgli sprang to his feet. "Free People," he cried, "does Shere Khan lead the pack? What has a tiger to do with our leadership?"

"Seeing that the leadership is yet open, and being asked to speak—" Shere Khan began.

"By whom?" said Mowgli. "Are we *all* jackals, to fawn on this cattle butcher? The leadership of the pack is with the pack alone."

There were yells of "Silence, thou man's cub!" "Let him speak. He has kept our Law." And at last the seniors of the pack thundered: "Let the Dead Wolf speak." When a leader of the pack has missed his kill, he is called the Dead Wolf as long as he lives, which is not long.

Akela raised his old head wearily:

"Free People, and ye too, jackals of Shere Khan, for twelve seasons I have led ye to and from the kill, and in all that time not one has been trapped or maimed. Now I have missed my kill. Ye know how that plot was made. Ye know how ye brought me up to an untried buck to make my weakness known. It was cleverly done. Your right is to kill me here on the Council Rock, now. Therefore, I ask, who comes to make an end of the Lone Wolf? For it is my right, by the Law of the Jungle, that ye come one by one."

There was a long hush, for no single wolf cared to fight Akela to the death. Then Shere Khan roared: "*Bah!* What have we to do with this toothless fool? He is doomed to die! It is the man-cub who has lived too long. Free People, he was my meat from the first. Give him to me. I am weary of this man-wolf folly. He has troubled the jungle for ten seasons. Give me the man-cub, or I will hunt here always, and not give you one bone. He is a man, a man's child, and from the marrow of my bones I hate him!"

Then more than half the pack yelled: "A man! A man! What has a man to do with us? Let him go to his own place."

"And turn all the people of the villages against us?" clamoured Shere Khan. "No! Give him to me. He is a man, and none of us can look him between the eyes."

Akela lifted his head again, and said: "He has eaten our food. He has slept with us. He has driven game for us. He has broken no word of the Law of the Jungle."

"Also, I paid for him with a bull when he was accepted. The worth of a bull is little, but Bagheera's honour is something that he will perhaps fight for," said Bagheera, in his gentlest voice.

"A bull paid ten years ago!" the pack snarled. "What do we care for bones ten years old?"

"Or for a pledge?" said Bagheera, his white teeth bared under his lip. "Well are ye called the Free People!"

"No man's cub can run with the people of the jungle," howled Shere Khan. "Give him to me!"

"He is our brother in all but blood," Akela went on, "and ye would kill him here! In truth, I have lived too long. Some of ye are eaters of cattle, and of others I have heard that, under Shere Khan's teaching, ye go by dark night and snatch children from the villager's doorstep.

Therefore I know ye to be cowards, and it is to cowards I speak. It is certain that I must die, and my life is of no worth, or I would offer that in the man-cub's place. But for the sake of the honour of the pack—a little matter that by being without a leader ye have forgotten—I promise that if ye let the man-cub go to his own place, I will not, when my time comes to die, bare one tooth against ye. I will die without fighting. That will at least save the pack three lives. More I cannot do; but if ye will, I can save ye the shame that comes of killing a brother against whom there is no fault—a brother spoken for and bought into the pack according to the Law of the Jungle."

"He is a man—a man—a man!" snarled the pack. And most of the wolves began to gather round Shere Khan, whose tail was beginning to switch.

"Now the business is in thy hands," said Bagheera to Mowgli. "*We* can do no more except fight."

Mowgli stood upright, the fire-pot in his hands. Then he stretched out his arms, and yawned in the face of the council. But he was furious with rage and sorrow, for, wolf-like, the wolves had never told him how they hated him. "Listen you!" he cried. "There is no need for this dog's jabber. Ye have told me so often tonight that I am a man (and indeed I would have been a wolf with you to my life's end), that I feel your words are true. So I do not call ye my brothers any more, but *sag* [dogs], as a man should. What ye will do, and what ye will not do, is not yours to say. That matter is with *me*. And that we may see the matter more plainly, I, the man, have brought here a little of the Red Flower which ye, dogs, fear."

He flung the fire-pot on the ground, and some of the red coals lit a tuft of dried moss that flared up, as all the council drew back in terror before the leaping flames.

Mowgli thrust his dead branch into the fire till the twigs lit and crackled, and whirled it above his head among the cowering wolves.

"Thou art the master," said Bagheera, in an undertone. "Save Akela from the death. He was ever thy friend."

Akela, the grim old wolf who had never asked for mercy in his life, gave one piteous look at Mowgli as the boy stood all naked, his long black hair tossing over his shoulders in the light of the blazing branch that made the shadows jump and quiver.

"Good!" said Mowgli, staring round slowly. "I see that ye are dogs. I go from you to my own people—if they be my own people. The jungle is shut to me, and I must forget your talk and your companionship; but I will be more merciful than ye are. Because I was all but your brother in blood, I promise that when I am a man among men I will not betray ye to men as ye have betrayed me." He kicked the fire with his foot, and the sparks flew up. "There shall be no war between any of us in the pack. But here is a debt to pay before I go." He strode forward to where Shere Khan sat blinking stupidly at the flames, and caught him by the tuft on his chin. Bagheera followed in case of accidents. "Up, dog!" Mowgli cried. "Up, when a man speaks, or I will set that coat ablaze!"

Shere Khan's ears lay flat back on his head, and he shut his eyes, for the blazing branch was very near.

"This cattle killer said he would kill me in the council because he had not killed me when I was a cub. Thus and thus, then, do we beat dogs when we are men. Stir a whisker, Lungri, and I ram the Red Flower down thy gullet!" He beat Shere Khan over the head with the branch, and the tiger whimpered and whined in an agony of fear.

"*Pah!* Singed jungle-cat—go now! But remember when next I come to the Council Rock, as a man should come, it will be with Shere Khan's hide on my head. For the rest, Akela goes free to live as he pleases. Ye will *not* kill him, because that is not my will. Nor do I think that ye will sit here any longer, lolling out your tongues as though ye were somebodies, instead of dogs whom I drive out—thus! Go!" The fire was burning furiously at the end of the branch, and Mowgli struck right and left round the circle, and the wolves ran howling with the sparks burning their fur. At last there were only Akela, Bagheera, and perhaps ten wolves that had taken Mowgli's part. Then something began to hurt Mowgli inside him, as he had never been hurt in his life before, and he caught his breath and sobbed, and the tears ran down his face.

"What is it? What is it?" he said. "I do not wish to leave the jungle, and I do not know what this is. Am I dying, Bagheera?"

"No, Little Brother. That is only tears such as men use," said Bagheera. "Now I know thou art a man, and a man's cub no longer. The jungle is shut indeed to thee henceforward. Let them fall, Mowgli. They are only tears." So Mowgli sat and cried as though his heart would break; and he had never cried in all his life before.

"Now," he said, "I will go to men. But first I must say farewell to my mother." And he went to the cave where she lived with Father Wolf, and he cried on her coat, while the four cubs howled miserably.

"Ye will not forget me?" said Mowgli.

"Never while we can follow a trail," said the cubs. "Come to the foot of the hill when thou art a man, and we will talk to thee; and we will come into the crop lands to play with thee by night."

"Come soon!" said Father Wolf. "Oh, wise little frog, come again soon, for we be old, thy mother and I."

"Come soon," said Mother Wolf, "little naked son of mine, for, listen, child of man, I loved thee more than ever I loved my cubs."

"I will surely come," said Mowgli, "and when I come it will be to lay out Shere Khan's hide upon the Council Rock. Do not forget me! Tell them in the jungle never to forget me!"

The dawn was beginning to break when Mowgli went down the hillside alone, to meet those mysterious things that are called men.

"TIGER-TIGER!"

Rudyard Kipling

When Mowgli left the wolf's cave after the fight with the pack at the Council Rock, he went down to the ploughed lands where the villagers lived, but he would not stop there because it was too near to the jungle, and he knew that he had made at least one bad enemy at the council. So he hurried on, keeping to the rough road that ran down the valley, and followed it at a steady jog trot for nearly twenty miles, till he came to a country that he did not know. The valley opened out into a great plain dotted over with rocks and cut up with ravines. At one end stood a little village, and at the other the thick jungle came down in a sweep to the grazing grounds, and stopped there as though it had been cut off with a hoe. All over the plain, cattle and buffaloes were grazing, and when the little boys in charge of the herds saw Mowgli they shouted and ran away, and the yellow pariah dogs that hang about every Indian village barked. Mowgli walked on, for he was feeling hungry, and when he came to the village gate he saw the big thornbush that was drawn up before the gate at twilight pushed to one side.

"Umph!" he said, for he had come across more than one such barricade in his night rambles after things to eat. "So men are afraid of the people of the jungle here also." He sat down by the gate, and when a man came out he stood up, opened his mouth, and pointed down it to show that he wanted food. The man stared, and ran back up the one street of the village shouting for the priest, who was a big, fat man dressed in white, with a red and yellow mark on his forehead. The priest came to the gate, and with him at least a hundred people, who stared and talked and shouted and pointed at Mowgli.

"They have no manners, these Men-Folk," said Mowgli to himself. "Only the grey ape would behave as they do." So he threw back his long hair and frowned at the crowd.

"What is there to be afraid of?" said the priest. "Look at the marks on his arms and legs. They are the bites of wolves. He is but a wolf-child run away from the jungle."

Of course, in playing together, the cubs had often nipped Mowgli harder than they intended, and there were white scars all over his arms and legs. But he would have been the last person in the world to call these bites, for he knew what real biting meant.

"Arré! Arré!" said two or three women together. "To be bitten by wolves, poor child! He is a handsome boy.

He has eyes like red fire. By my honour, Messua, he is not unlike thy boy that was taken by the tiger."

"Let me look," said a woman with heavy copper rings on her wrists and ankles, and she peered at Mowgli under the palm of her hand. "Indeed he is not. He is thinner, but he has the very look of my boy."

The priest was a clever man, and he knew that Messua was wife to the richest villager in the place. So he looked up at the sky for a minute, and said solemnly: "What the jungle has taken the jungle has restored. Take the boy into thy house, my sister, and forget not to honour the priest who sees so far into the lives of men."

"By the bull that bought me," said Mowgli to himself, "but all this talking is like another looking over by the pack! Well, if I am a man, a man I must be."

The crowd parted as the woman beckoned Mowgli to her hut, where there was a red lacquered bedstead, a great earthen grain chest with funny raised patterns on it, half a dozen copper cooking pots, an image of a Hindu god in a little alcove, and on the wall a real looking glass, such as they sell at the country fairs for eight cents.

She gave him a long drink of milk and some bread, and then she laid her hand on his head and looked into his eyes, for she thought perhaps that he might be her real son come back from the jungle where the tiger had taken him. So she said: "Nathoo, O Nathoo!" Mowgli did not show that he knew the name. "Dost thou not remember the day when I gave thee thy new shoes?" She touched his foot, and it was almost as hard as horn.

"No," she said, sorrowfully, "those feet have never worn shoes, but thou art very like my Nathoo, and thou shalt be my son."

Mowgli was uneasy, because he had never been under a roof before; but as he looked at the thatch, he saw that he could tear it out any time if he wanted to get away, and that the window had no fastenings. "What is the good of a man," he said to himself at last, "if he does not understand man's talk? Now I am as silly and dumb as a man would be with us in the jungle. I must speak their talk."

He had not learned while he was with the wolves to imitate the challenge of bucks in the jungle and the grunt of the little wild pig for fun. So, as soon as Messua pronounced a word Mowgli would imitate it almost perfectly, and before dark he had learned the name of many things in the hut.

There was a difficulty at bedtime, because Mowgli would not sleep under anything that looked so like a panther-trap as that hut, and when they shut the door he went through the window. "Give him his will," said Messua's husband. "Remember he can never till now have slept on a bed. If he is indeed sent in the place of our son he will not run away."

So Mowgli stretched himself in some long clean grass at the edge of the field, but before he had closed his eyes a soft grey nose poked him under the chin.

"Phew!" said Grey Brother (he was the eldest of Mother Wolf's cubs). "This is a poor reward for

following thee twenty miles. Thou smellest of wood smoke and cattle—altogether like a man already. Wake, Little Brother; I bring news."

"Are all well in the jungle?" said Mowgli, hugging him.

"All except the wolves that were burned with the Red Flower. Now, listen. Shere Khan has gone away to hunt far off till his coat grows again, for he is badly singed. When he returns he swears that he will lay thy bones in the Wainganga."

"There are two words to that. I also have made a little promise. But news is always good. I am tired tonight—very tired with new things, Grey Brother—but bring me the news always."

"Thou wilt not forget that thou art a wolf? Men will not make thee forget?" said Grey Brother, anxiously.

"Never. I will always remember that I love thee and all in our cave, but also I will always remember that I have been cast out of the pack."

"And that thou mayest be cast out of another pack. Men are only men, Little Brother, and their talk is like the talk of frogs in a pond. When I come down here again, I will wait for thee in the bamboos at the edge of the grazing ground."

For three months after that night Mowgli hardly ever left the village gate, he was so busy learning the ways and customs of men. First he had to wear a cloth round him, which annoyed him horribly; and then he had to learn about money, which he did not in the least understand,

and about ploughing, of which he did not see the use. Then the little children in the village made him very angry. Luckily, the Law of the Jungle had taught him to keep his temper, for in the jungle, life and food depend on keeping your temper; but when they made fun of him because he would not play games or fly kites, or because he mispronounced some word, only the knowledge that it was unsportsmanlike to kill little naked cubs kept him from picking them up and breaking them in two. He did not know his own strength in the least. In the jungle he knew he was weak compared with the beasts, but in the village, people said that he was as strong as a bull. He certainly had no notion of what fear was, for when the village priest told him that the god in the temple would be angry with him if he ate the priest's mangoes, he picked up the image, brought it over to the priest's house, and asked the priest to make the god angry and he would be happy to fight him. It was a horrible scandal, but the priest hushed it up, and Messua's husband paid much good silver to comfort the god. And Mowgli had not the faintest idea of the difference that caste makes between man and man. When the potter's donkey slipped in the clay pit, Mowgli hauled it out by the tail and helped to stack the pots for their journey to the market at Khanhiwara. That was very shocking, too, for the potter is a low-caste man, and his donkey is worse. When the priest scolded him, Mowgli threatened to put him on the donkey, too, and the priest told Messua's husband that Mowgli had better be set to work as soon as possible; and the village headman told Mowgli that he would have to go out with the buffaloes next day, and herd them while they grazed. No one was more pleased than Mowgli; and that night, because he had been appointed a servant of the village, as it were, he went off to a circle that met every evening on a masonry platform under a great fig tree. It was the village club, and the headman and the watchman and the barber, who knew all the gossip of the village, and old Buldeo, the village hunter, who had a Tower musket, met and smoked. The monkeys sat and talked in the upper branches, and there was a hole under the platform where a cobra lived, and he had his little platter of milk every night because he was sacred; and the old men sat around the tree and talked, and pulled at the big *huqas* (the water-pipes) till far into the night. They told wonderful tales of gods and men and ghosts; and Buldeo told even more wonderful ones of the ways of beasts in the jungle, till the eyes of the children sitting outside the circle bulged out of their heads. Most of the tales were about animals, for the jungle was always at their door. The deer and the wild pig grubbed up their crops, and now and again the tiger carried off a man at twilight, within sight of the village gates.

Mowgli, who naturally knew something about what they were talking of, had to cover his face not to show that he was laughing, while Buldeo, the Tower musket across his knees, climbed on from one wonderful story to another, and Mowgli's shoulders shook.

Buldeo was explaining how the tiger that had carried away Messua's son was a ghost-tiger, and his body was inhabited by the ghost of a wicked, old moneylender who had died some years ago. "And I know that this is true," he said, "because Purun Dass always limped from the blow that he got in a riot when his account books were burned, and the tiger that I speak of *he* limps, too, for the tracks of his pads are unequal."

"True, true, that must be the truth," said the greybeards nodding together.

"Are all these tales such cobwebs and moon-talk?" said Mowgli. "That tiger limps because he was born lame, as everyone knows. To talk of the soul of a moneylender in a beast that never had the courage of a jackal is child's talk."

Buldeo was speechless with surprise for a moment, and the headman stared.

"Oho! It is the jungle brat, is it?" said Buldeo. "If thou art so wise, better bring his hide to Khanhiwara, for the Government has set a hundred rupees on his life. Better still, talk not when thy elders speak."

Mowgli rose to go. "All the evening I have lain here listening," he called back, over his shoulder, "and, except once or twice, Buldeo has not said one word of truth concerning the jungle, which is at his very doors. How then shall I believe the tales of ghosts, and gods, and goblins which he says he has seen?"

"It is full time that boy went to herding," said the headman, while Buldeo puffed and snorted at Mowgli's impertinence.

The custom of most Indian villages is for a few boys to take the cattle and buffaloes out to graze in the early morning, and bring them back at night; and the very cattle that would trample a white man to death allow themselves to be banged and bullied and shouted at by children that hardly come up to their noses. So long as the boys keep with the herds they are safe, for not even the tiger will charge a mob of cattle. But if they straggle to pick flowers or hunt lizards, they are sometimes carried off. Mowgli went through the village street in the dawn, sitting on the back of Rama, the great herd bull; and the slaty-blue buffaloes, with their long, backward-sweeping horns and savage eyes, rose out of their byres, one by one, and followed him, and Mowgli made it very clear to the children with him that he was the master. He beat the buffaloes with a long, polished bamboo, and told Kamya, one of the boys, to graze the cattle by themselves, while he went on with the buffaloes, and to be very careful not to stray away from the herd.

An Indian grazing ground is all rocks, and scrubs, and tussocks, and little ravines, among which the herds scatter and disappear. The buffaloes generally keep to the pools and muddy places, where they lie wallowing or basking in the warm mud for hours. Mowgli drove them on to the edge of the plain where the Wainganga came out of the jungle; then he dropped from Rama's neck, trotted off to a bamboo clump, and found Grey Brother. "Ah," said Grey Brother, "I have waited here very many days. What is the meaning of this cattle-herding work?"

"It is an order," said Mowgli. "I am a village herder for a while. What news of Shere Khan?"

"He has come back to this country, and has waited here a long time for thee. Now he has gone off again, for the game is scarce. But he means to kill thee."

"Very good," said Mowgli. "So long as he is away do thou or one of the four brothers sit on that rock, so that I can see thee as I come out of the village. When he comes back, wait for me in the ravine by the *dhâk*-tree in the centre of the plain. We need not walk into Shere Khan's mouth."

Then Mowgli picked out a shady place, and lay down and slept while the buffaloes grazed round him. Herding in India is one of the laziest things in the world. The cattle move and crunch, and lie down, and move on again, and they do not even low. They only grunt, and the buffaloes very seldom say anything, but get down into the muddy pools one after another, and work their way into the mud till only their noses and staring china-blue eyes show above the surface, and then they lie like logs. The sun makes the rocks dance in the heat, and the herd-children hear one kite (never any more) whistling almost out of sight overhead, and they know that if they died, or a cow died, that kite would sweep down, and the next kite miles away would see him drop and follow, and the next, and the next, and almost before they were dead there would be a score of hungry kites come out of nowhere. Then they sleep and wake and sleep again, and weave little baskets of dried grass and put grasshoppers in them, or catch two praying mantises and make them fight, or string a necklace of red and black jungle-nuts, or watch a lizard basking on a rock, or a snake hunting a frog near the wallows. Then they sing long, long songs with odd native quavers at the end of them, and the day seems longer than most people's whole lives, and perhaps they make a mud castle with mud figures of men and horses and buffaloes, and put reeds into the men's hands, and pretend that they are kings and the figures are their armies, or that they are gods to be worshipped. Then evening comes and the children call, and the buffaloes lumber up out of the sticky mud with noises like gunshots going off one after the other, and they all string across the grey plain back to the twinkling village lights.

Day after day Mowgli would lead the buffaloes out to their wallows, and day after day he would see Grey Brother's back a mile and a half away across the plain (so he knew that Shere Khan had not come back), and day after day he would lie on the grass listening to the noises round him, and dreaming of old days in the jungle. If Shere Khan had made a false step with his lame paw up in the jungles by the Wainganga, Mowgli would have heard him in those long still mornings.

At last a day came when he did not see Grey Brother at the signal place, and he laughed and headed the buffaloes for the ravine by the *dhâk*-tree, which was all covered with golden-red flowers. There sat Grey Brother, every bristle on his back lifted.

"He has hidden for a month to throw thee off thy guard. He crossed the ranges last night with Tabaqui, hot-foot on thy trail," said the wolf, panting.

Mowgli frowned. "I am not afraid of Shere Khan, but Tabaqui is very cunning."

"Have no fear," said Grey Brother, licking his lips a little. "I met Tabaqui in the dawn. Now he is telling all his wisdom to the kites, but he told *me* everything before I broke his back. Shere Khan's plan is to wait for thee at the village gate this evening—for thee and for no one else. He is lying up now, in the big dry ravine of the Wainganga."

"Has he eaten today, or does he hunt empty?" said Mowgli, for the answer meant life and death to him.

"He killed at dawn—a pig—and he has drunk too. Remember, Shere Khan could never fast, even for the sake of revenge."

"Oh! Fool, fool! What a cub's cub it is! Eaten and drunk too, and he thinks that I shall wait till he has slept! Now, where does he lie up? If there were but ten of us we might pull him down as he lies. These buffaloes will not charge unless they wind him, and I cannot speak their language. Can we get behind his track so that they may smell it?"

"He swam far down the Wainganga to cut that off," said Grey Brother.

"Tabaqui told him that, I know. He would never have thought of it alone." Mowgli stood with his finger in his mouth, thinking. "The big ravine of the Wainganga.

That opens out on the plain not half a mile from here. I can take the herd round through the jungle to the head of the ravine and then sweep down—but he would slink out at the foot. We must block that end. Grey Brother, canst thou cut the herd in two for me?"

"Not I, perhaps—but I have brought a wise helper." Grey Brother trotted off and dropped into a hole. Then there lifted up a huge grey head that Mowgli knew well, and the hot air was filled with the most desolate cry of all the jungle—the hunting-howl of a wolf at midday.

"Akela! Akela!" said Mowgli, clapping his hands. "I might have known that thou wouldst not forget me. We have a big work in hand. Cut the herd in two, Akela. Keep the cows and calves together, and the bulls and the plough-buffaloes by themselves."

The two wolves ran, ladies'-chain fashion, in and out of the herd, which snorted and threw up its head, and separated into two clumps. In one, the cow-buffaloes stood with their calves in the centre, and glared and pawed, ready, if a wolf would only stay still, to charge down and trample the life out of him. In the other, the bulls and the young bulls snorted and stamped, but though they looked more imposing they were much less dangerous, for they had no calves to protect. No six men could have divided the herd so neatly.

"What orders!" panted Akela. "They are trying to join again."

Mowgli slipped onto Rama's back. "Drive the bulls away to the left, Akela. Grey Brother, when we are gone, hold the cows together, and drive them into the foot of the ravine."

"How far?" said Grey Brother, panting and snapping.

"Till the sides are higher than Shere Khan can jump," shouted Mowgli. "Keep them there till we come down." The bulls swept off as Akela bayed, and Grey Brother stopped in front of the cows. They charged down on him, and he ran just before them to the foot of the ravine, as Akela drove the bulls far to the left.

"Well done! Another charge and they are fairly started. Careful, now—careful, Akela. A snap too much, and the bulls will charge. *Hujah!* This is wilder work than driving black-buck. Didst thou think these creatures could move so swiftly?" Mowgli called.

"I have—have hunted these too in my time," gasped Akela in the dust. "Shall I turn them into the jungle?"

"Aye! Turn. Swiftly turn them! Rama is mad with rage. Oh, if I could only tell him what I need of him today."

The bulls were turned, to the right this time, and crashed into the standing thicket. The other herd-children, watching with the cattle half a mile away, hurried to the village as fast as their legs could carry them, crying that the buffaloes had gone mad and run away. But Mowgli's plan was simple enough. All he wanted to do was to make a big circle uphill and get at the head of the ravine, and then take the bulls down it and catch Shere Khan between the bulls and the cows, for he knew that after a meal and a full drink Shere Khan would not be in any condition to fight or to clamber up the sides of the ravine. He was soothing the buffaloes now by voice, and Akela had dropped far to the rear, only whimpering once or twice to hurry the rear guard. It was a long, long circle, for they did not wish to get too near the ravine and give Shere Khan warning. At last Mowgli rounded up the bewildered herd at the head of the ravine on a grassy patch that sloped steeply down to the ravine itself. From that height you could see across the tops of the trees down to the plain below; but what Mowgli looked at was the sides of the ravine, and he saw with a great deal of satisfaction that they ran nearly straight up and down, while the vines and creepers that hung over them would give no foothold to a tiger who wanted to get out.

"Let them breathe, Akela," he said, holding up his hand. "They have not winded him yet. Let them breathe. I must tell Shere Khan who comes. We have him in the trap."

He put his hands to his mouth and shouted down the ravine—it was almost like shouting down a tunnel—and the echoes jumped from rock to rock.

After a long time there came back the drawling, sleepy snarl of a full-fed tiger just wakened.

"Who calls?" said Shere Khan, and a splendid peacock fluttered up out of the ravine screeching.

"I, Mowgli. Cattle thief, it is time to come to the Council Rock! Down—hurry them down, Akela! Down, Rama, down!"

The herd paused for an instant at the edge of the slope, but Akela gave tongue in the full hunting yell, and they pitched over one after the other just as steamers shoot rapids, the sand and stones spurting up round them. Once started, there was no chance of stopping, and before they were fairly in the bed of the ravine Rama winded Shere Khan and bellowed.

"Ha! Ha!" said Mowgli, on his back. "Now thou knowest!" And the torrent of black horns, foaming muzzles, and staring eyes whirled down the ravine just as boulders go down in flood-time, the weaker buffaloes being shouldered out to the sides of the ravine where they tore through the creepers. They knew what the business was before them—the terrible charge of the buffalo herd against which no tiger can hope to stand. Shere Khan heard the thunder of their hoofs, picked himself up, and lumbered down the ravine, looking from side to side for some way of escape, but the walls of the ravine were straight and he had to hold on, heavy with his dinner and his drink, willing to do anything rather than fight. The herd splashed through the pool he had just left, bellowing till the narrow cut rang. Mowgli heard an answering bellow from the foot of the ravine, saw Shere Khan turn (the tiger knew if the worst came to the worst it was better to meet the bulls than the cows with their calves), and then Rama tripped, stumbled, and went on again over something soft, and, with the bulls at his heels, crashed full into the other herd, while the weaker buffaloes were lifted clean off their feet by the shock of the meeting. That charge carried both herds out into the plain, goring and stamping and snorting. Mowgli watched his time, and slipped off Rama's neck, laying about him right and left with his stick.

"Quick, Akela! Break them up. Scatter them, or they will be fighting one another. Drive them away, Akela. *Hai,* Rama! *Hai! hai! hai!* my children. Softly now, softly! It is all over."

Akela and Grey Brother ran to and fro nipping the buffaloes' legs, and though the herd wheeled once to charge up the ravine again, Mowgli managed to turn Rama, and the others followed him to the wallows.

Shere Khan needed no more trampling. He was dead, and the kites were coming for him already.

"Brothers, that was a dog's death," said Mowgli, feeling for the knife he always carried in a sheath round his neck now that he lived with men. "But he would never have shown fight. *Wallah!* His hide will look well on the Council Rock. We must get to work swiftly."

A boy trained among men would never have dreamed of skinning a ten-foot tiger alone, but Mowgli knew better than anyone else how an animal's skin is fitted on, and how it can be taken off. But it was hard work, and Mowgli slashed and tore and grunted for an hour, while the wolves lolled out their tongues, or came forward and tugged as he ordered them. Presently a hand fell on his shoulder, and looking up he saw Buldeo with the Tower musket. The children had told the village about the buffalo stampede, and Buldeo went out angrily, only too anxious to correct Mowgli for not taking better care of the herd. The wolves dropped out of sight as soon as they saw the man coming.

"What is this folly?" said Buldeo, angrily. "To think that thou canst skin a tiger! Where did the buffaloes kill him? It is the Lame Tiger, too, and there is a hundred rupees on his head. Well, well, we will overlook thy letting the herd run off, and perhaps I will give thee one of the rupees of the reward when I have taken the skin to Khanhiwara." He fumbled in his waist-cloth for flint and steel, and stooped down to singe Shere Khan's whiskers. Most native hunters always singe a tiger's whiskers to prevent his ghost from haunting them.

"Hum!" said Mowgli, half to himself, as he ripped back the skin of a forepaw. "So thou wilt take the hide to Khanhiwara for the reward, and perhaps give me one rupee? Now it is in my mind that I need the skin for my own use. *Heh!* Old man, take away that fire!"

"What talk is this to the chief hunter of the village? Thy luck and the stupidity of thy buffaloes have helped thee to this kill. The tiger has just fed, or he would have gone twenty miles by this time. Thou canst not even skin him properly, little beggar brat, and forsooth I, Buldeo, must be told not to singe his whiskers. Mowgli, I will not give thee one anna of the reward, but only a very big beating. Leave the carcass!"

"By the bull that bought me," said Mowgli, who was trying to get at the shoulder, "must I stay babbling to an old ape all noon? Here, Akela, this man plagues me."

Buldeo, who was still stooping over Shere Khan's head, found himself sprawling on the grass, with a grey wolf standing over him, while Mowgli went on skinning as though he were alone in all India.

"Ye-es," he said, between his teeth. "Thou art altogether right, Buldeo. Thou wilt never give me one anna of the reward. There is an old war between this lame tiger and myself—a very old war, and—I have won."

To do Buldeo justice, if he had been ten years younger he would have taken his chance with Akela had he met the wolf in the woods, but a wolf who obeyed the orders of this boy who had private wars with man-eating tigers was not a common animal. It was sorcery, magic of the worst kind, thought Buldeo, and he wondered whether the amulet round his neck would protect him. He lay as still as still, expecting every minute to see Mowgli turn into a tiger, too.

"Maharaj! Great King," he said at last, in a husky whisper.

"Yes," said Mowgli, without turning his head, chuckling a little.

"I am an old man. I did not know that thou wast anything more than a herdsboy. May I rise up and go away, or will thy servant tear me to pieces?"

"Go, and peace go with thee. Only, another time do not meddle with my game. Let him go, Akela."

Buldeo hobbled away to the village as fast as he could, looking back over his shoulder in case Mowgli should change into something terrible. When he got to the village he told a tale of magic and enchantment and sorcery that made the priest look very grave.

Mowgli went on with his work, but it was nearly twilight before he and the wolves had drawn the great gay skin clear of the body.

"Now we must hide this and take the buffaloes home! Help me to herd them, Akela."

The herd rounded up in the misty twilight, and when they got near the village Mowgli saw lights, and heard the conches and bells in the temple blowing and banging. Half the village seemed to be waiting for him by the gate. "That is because I have killed Shere Khan," he said to himself. But a shower of stones whistled about his ears, and the villagers shouted: "Sorcerer! Wolf's-brat! Jungle-demon! Go away! Get hence quickly, or the priest will turn thee into a wolf again. Shoot, Buldeo, shoot!"

The old Tower musket went off with a bang, and a young buffalo bellowed in pain.

"More sorcery!" shouted the villagers. "He can turn bullets. Buldeo, that was *thy* buffalo."

"Now what is this?" said Mowgli, bewildered, as the stones flew thicker.

"They are not unlike the pack, these brothers of thine," said Akela, sitting down composedly. "It is in my head that, if bullets mean anything, they would cast thee out."

"Wolf! Wolf's cub! Go away!" shouted the priest, waving a sprig of the sacred *tulsi* plant.

"Again? Last time it was because I was a man. This time it is because I am a wolf. Let us go, Akela."

A woman—it was Messua—ran across to the herd, and cried: "Oh, my son, my son! They say thou art a sorcerer who can turn himself into a beast at will. I do not believe, but go away or they will kill thee. Buldeo says thou art a wizard, but I know thou hast avenged Nathoo's death."

"Come back, Messua!" shouted the crowd. "Come back, or we will stone thee."

Mowgli laughed a little short ugly laugh, for a stone had hit him in the mouth. "Run back, Messua. This is one of the foolish tales they tell under the big tree at dusk. I have at least paid for thy son's life. Farewell, and run quickly, for I shall send the herd in more swiftly than their brickbats. I am no wizard, Messua. Farewell!"

"Now, once more, Akela," he cried. "Bring the herd in."

The buffaloes were anxious enough to get to the village. They hardly needed Akela's yell, but charged through the gate like a whirlwind, scattering the crowd right and left.

"Keep count!" shouted Mowgli, scornfully. "It may be that I have stolen one of them. Keep count, for I will do your herding no more. Fare you well, children of men, and thank Messua that I do not come in with my wolves and hunt you up and down your street."

He turned on his heel and walked away with the Lone Wolf, and as he looked up at the stars he felt happy. "No more sleeping in traps for me, Akela. Let us get Shere Khan's skin and go away. No, we will not hurt the village, for Messua was kind to me."

When the moon rose over the plain, making it look all milky, the horrified villagers saw Mowgli, with two wolves at his heels and a bundle on his head, trotting across at the steady wolf's trot that eats up the long miles like fire. Then they banged the temple bells and blew the conches louder than ever. And Messua cried, and Buldeo embroidered the story of his adventures in the jungle, till he ended by saying that Akela stood up on his hind legs and talked like a man.

The moon was just going down when Mowgli and the two wolves came to the hill of the Council Rock, and they stopped at Mother Wolf's cave.

"They have cast me out from the man pack, Mother," shouted Mowgli, "but I come with the hide of Shere Khan to keep my word." Mother Wolf walked stiffly from the cave with the cubs behind her, and her eyes glowed as she saw the skin.

"I told him on that day, when he crammed his head and shoulders into this cave, hunting for thy life, little frog—I told him that the hunter would be the hunted. It is well done."

"Little Brother, it is well done," said a deep voice in the thicket. "We were lonely in the jungle without thee," and Bagheera came running to Mowgli's bare feet.

They clambered up the Council Rock together, and Mowgli spread the skin out on the flat stone where Akela used to sit, and pegged it down with four slivers of bamboo, and Akela lay down upon it, and called the old call to the council: "Look, look well, O wolves," exactly as he had called when Mowgli was first brought there.

Ever since Akela had been deposed, the pack had been without a leader, hunting and fighting at their own pleasure. But they answered the call from habit, and some of them were lame from the traps they had fallen into, and some limped from shot-wounds, and some were mangy from eating bad food, and many were missing. But they came to the Council Rock, all that were left of them, and saw Shere Khan's striped hide on the rock, and the huge claws dangling at the end of the empty dangling feet.

"Look well, O wolves. Have I kept my word?" said Mowgli. And the wolves bayed Yes, and one tattered wolf howled:

"Lead us again, O Akela. Lead us again, O man-cub, for we be sick of this lawlessness, and we would be the Free People once more."

"Nay," purred Bagheera, "that may not be. When ye are full-fed, the madness may come upon you again. Not for nothing are ye called the Free People. Ye fought for freedom, and it is yours. Eat it, O wolves."

"Man pack and wolf pack have cast me out," said Mowgli. "Now I will hunt alone in the jungle."

"And we will hunt with thee," said the four cubs.

So Mowgli went away and hunted with the four cubs in the jungle from that day on. But he was not always alone, because, years afterward, he became a man and married.

But that is a story for grownups.

ACKNOWLEDGMENTS

All possible care has been taken to trace ownership and secure permission for each selection in this series. The Great Books Foundation wishes to thank the following authors, publishers, and representatives for permission to reprint copyrighted material:

A Game of Catch, by Richard Wilbur. Copyright 1953, 1981 by The New Yorker Magazine, Inc. Reprinted by permission of The New Yorker Magazine, Inc.

The Tale of the Three Storytellers, from MY GREAT-GRANDFATHER AND I, by James Krüss. Translation copyright 1964 by Atheneum Publishers. Reprinted by permission of Atheneum Publishers, an imprint of Macmillan Publishing Company.

Spit Nolan, from THE GOALKEEPER'S REVENGE AND OTHER STORIES, by Bill Naughton. Copyright 1961 by Bill Naughton. Reprinted by permission of Peters, Fraser & Dunlop Limited.

The Queen's Care, from SERENDIPITY TALES, by Elizabeth Jamison Hodges. Copyright 1966 by Elizabeth Jamison Hodges. Reprinted by permission of McIntosh and Otis Inc.

Lucky Boy, from WHAT THE NEIGHBOURS DID AND OTHER STORIES, by Philippa Pearce. Copyright 1959, 1967, 1969, 1972 by Philippa Pearce. Reprinted by permission of Penguin Books Limited.

The Secret of the Hattifatteners, from TALES FROM MOOMINVALLEY, by Tove Jansson. Translation copyright 1963 by Ernest Benn Limited. Reprinted by permission of A & C Black (Publishers) Limited.

Kaddo's Wall, from THE COW-TAIL SWITCH AND OTHER WEST AFRICAN STORIES, by Harold Courlander and George Herzog. Copyright 1947 by Henry Holt and Company, Inc. Copyright 1975 by Harold Courlander and George Herzog. Copyright 1986 by Harold Courlander. Reprinted by permission of Henry Holt and Company, Inc.

Dita's Story, from THE OWL'S KISS, by Mary Q. Steele. Copyright 1978 by Mary Q. Steele. Reprinted by permission of William Morrow & Company, Inc.

Oliver Hyde's Dishcloth Concert, from RICHARD KENNEDY: COLLECTED STORIES. Copyright 1977 by Richard Kennedy. Reprinted by permission of the author.

ILLUSTRATION CREDITS

Tove Jansson's illustrations for *The Secret of the Hattifatteners* are from TALES FROM MOOMINVALLEY. Illustrations copyright 1962 by Tove Jansson. Reprinted by permission of A & C Black (Publishers) Limited.

Cover art and title page illustration by Ed Young. Copyright 1992 by Ed Young. Title page illustration is based on *The Tale of the Three Storytellers.*

Text and cover design by William Seabright,
William Seabright & Associates.